THE DARK INSIDE

RUPERT WALLIS

SIMON&SCHUSTER

First published in Great Britain in 2014 by Simon and Schuster UK Ltd
A CBS COMPANY

This paperback edition published in 2014

1 3 5 7 9 10 8 6 4 2

Simon & Schuster UK Ltd
1st Floor, 222 Gray's Inn Road
London
WC1X 8HB

Simon & Schuster Australia, Sydney
Simon & Schuster India, New Delhi

A CIP catalogue record for this book is available from the British Library.

PB ISBN: 978-1-4711-1889-0
EBook ISBN: 978-1-4711-1890-6

Printed and bound by CPI Group (UK) Ltd, Croydon, CR0 4YY

www.simonandschuster.co.uk
www.simonandschuster.com.au

For my mother.

And for my father (wherever he may or may not be).

Homo sapiens

Latin for wise or knowing man

June 8th

1

Run.

And James did. Out the back door. Through the gap in the garden fence. Not stopping even after the bellowing of his stepfather had wasted in the wind and there was nothing but the whip of grass across his shins.

He cut a silver channel through the meadow . . .

. . . climbed the rotten, spongy stile . . .

. . . dropped down into the lane and kept on going, fists pumping as the slope began to bite.

The 'house on the hill' it was called. A small lead box on the skyline at a couple of miles. Inside, it was a musty, cobwebby place with peeling walls slick from damp. It had been there on the hill overlooking the village for as long as anyone could remember. Ever-present. Like a boulder left over from an ancient time.

The kitchen was cool and smelt of sea spray.

James leant against the old range cooker to catch his breath. His arm was sore, below the sleeve of his T-shirt, where his stepfather had punched him. James had not dropped the bottle. But his stepfather found it much easier to blame the boy for things.

A bruise was darkening and rubbing only made it worse and more difficult to forget. So he walked on into a large hallway and stopped at the bottom of a wooden staircase with a wide, pale stripe up its centre. He waited, listening, until he was sure he was alone, then carried on up the stairs, accompanied by a tune of creaks and clicks he knew off by heart.

Up on to the landing . . .

. . . then straight on into a large bedroom.

Rotten bay windows.

Green hills beyond.

A stub of chalk below them on the window sill.

The long wall opposite was painted black with writing chalked all over that winked like frost. Wrapping his hand inside his T-shirt, James wiped away the final digit from a number written large in the centre of the wall that read

1,642

and rewrote it as

1,641

He mouthed the number like a prayer, shuffling backwards, then slumping down on the baggy green sofa behind him in a cloud of dust and sunlight. The fabric smelt, but the boy put up with it because the house was somewhere to be.

He sat for a while, staring at the writing on the wall. And then he sighed and stood up, and placed the chalk back on the window sill and looked out at the canopy of blue sky overhanging the green hills.

Sheep were grubs.

A bird circling in the blue became a taut black line.

He walked slowly round the top floor of the house, inspecting each room carefully in turn, because he was in no hurry to go home. Which was why he found the body. It was lying against a wall in the smallest of the five bedrooms.

As if the sea had left it there for him to find.

2

It was wearing a blue wool greatcoat and black boots with eyelets and tractor-tyre soles. It was a man. Curled up into a ball on the wooden floor.

James stood, watching for any hint of breathing. Listening out for any sound. But there seemed to be no sign of life. So he stepped closer. Just to be sure.

The skin on the man's hands was so white it was blue. Below the black, oily hair was a gash the size of a mouth on his upturned cheek. Bruises the colour of storm clouds on his neck.

Something clicked behind him and James whirled round. But it was just the house, the walls and floorboards, ticking over in the afternoon sun.

When he looked down again, two blue eyes were staring up at him. James stepped back a few paces and stopped. When the man had been dead, there had been no need to think very hard.

The whole thing could have been a dream.

But it wasn't.

'I won't hurt you,' said the man. He was as weak as a kitten, his arms collapsing with the slightest weight, but he managed to prop himself up against the wall below the window, the sky all the bluer against his black hair. 'Where am I?'

'The house on the hill,' replied James. 'On the edge of Timpston,' he added. 'In Devon.'

'Falconbury?'

'About three miles away. Is that where you're from? The town?'

'No.'

Outside, the leaves suddenly started chattering as though some great current was coursing through the earth into the trees. The two of them stared silently at one another as if waiting for a terrible shock to reach them. And then the wind faded as quickly as it had begun.

Every note of James's voice had been sucked from his chest making it impossible to speak.

'I'll be fine.' The man curled up into a ball again. Closed his eyes. Coughed. And then lay still.

James backed all the way to the door.

Walked quickly down the stairs.

Left the house through the kitchen door.

He stood nearby, flashing a stick back and forth over a patch of young nettles, making them shiver. *He could be anyone*, thought James. *A homeless person. A prisoner on the run. Someone just down on their luck.*

I'll be fine.

Whoever he was, he didn't want any help.

The bruise on James's arm began to creak and groan and ache, and he stopped wondering about the man, and who he might be, and drove the stick harder.

Nettle heads flew.

Necks opened.

He mashed the stalks until the ground around him reeked of green.

3

'Where have you been?'

James dug the toe of his trainer into a gap between two paving stones on the patio. But it wouldn't open up and swallow him.

His stepfather was sitting on the kitchen step at the back of their house, smoking a cigarette, shirtsleeves rolled up into thick white bands. His forearms looked bulky and golden in the early evening sunlight. The smoke around him was a tangle of blue. 'Well?'

'Just walking about.'

'What? All this time? Just *walk-ing* about?'

James nodded, because it was always difficult to say the right thing. He tried following the song of a blackbird, and when he noticed the yellow washing line, strung between its poles, he tried to remember all the clothes that had ever hung there.

9

'What's that on your arm?' asked his stepfather, pointing at the bruise. The centre had become as black as coal, the rest of it raw and purple with mottling around the edges.

'Nothing. I'll be fine.'

'Course you will.' The cigarette glowed orange. 'Course. You. Will.'

I'll be fine. That's what James had said. He knew he wasn't. But it was what people said all the time. It was what the man in the house had said too.

He was lying in bed under a single white sheet, staring up at the ceiling. Sweat crackled on his brow and in the dark private pits of his body. His tongue rang with salt and pepper each time he licked his lips and tried to think everything through.

The man was not all right.

He kicked back the sheet. Peered out of the window into the grainy dark.

In the distance the house on the hill was blacker than the night sky.

James knew what his mother would have done. He wondered if she might be watching him now, waiting to see what he would do. He hoped she was, and whispered to her, asking that she forgive him for not visiting her grave as often as he should. And then for all the other things she might be watching out for too.

But the man could be anyone.

He got out of bed.

Dressed quietly.

After finding the torch in the bottom of his wardrobe, he lit a spot on the wall and ran the light around the room. They had chosen the striped blue wallpaper together. And the porthole mirror. Even the chest of drawers opposite the bed.

The light caught the glass and then the photograph of her in the little brown frame. She was smiling right at him.

James clicked off the torch. For a moment, it felt just like the car accident all over again, until his eyes adjusted to the dark.

4

The church clock struck half past eleven.

James clicked the front door shut as gently as he could, knowing his stepfather would be sitting on the back step by now, smoking like he did every night, after the pub had finished serving.

But, walking the long way through the village to get to the bottom of the hill, he was surprised to see the windows in the bar of the pub still glowing. So he crossed to the other side of the street, staying in the shadows, wary of the laughter inside. When the door opened, he saw his stepfather, lit like an angel, before the man dipped his head and cupped his hands to suck alight a cigarette. The match hit the pavement with a tiny clink and died. And something inside James did too as he tried to understand why his stepfather was not at home.

A woman with long blonde hair tottered into the doorway and when she placed a hand on the man's shoulder to steady herself the two of them laughed. Then they left the pub and began crossing the road. James pulled back into the alleyway behind him and crouched down in the gloom, holding his breath, hoping for the world to keep on turning.

Their voices were loose and loud. Stilettos rang. His stepfather raised his arms like the wings of a bird. When they reached the pavement, the woman stumbled on the kerb and his stepfather caught her, and they kissed and became one shape in the dark, the cigarette glowing like a red moon in orbit around them.

James heard his heart and worried it would give him away. He shuffled further back into the dark of the alley, the soles of his trainers rolling the grit beneath him.

The kissing stopped.

'Who's that?' asked his stepfather, his voice rosy and golden with beer. 'Come on out!'

The woman giggled.

'My hero,' she said. 'My brave boy.' But, when she touched him on the shoulder, he shrugged her hand away and his body stiffened like a sail. He took a big drag on his cigarette and threw it down and ground it out.

'Come on out here. Now!'

The woman looked away when she saw James. And then she turned back and whispered something and his stepfather nodded. Sighed. And folded his arms.

She walked back across the road towards the pub, her heels clicking out of time, until she opened the door. Glasses were being stacked. Somebody laughed. And then she pulled the door shut behind her.

James heard his breath rising and falling in his chest.

'What were you doing spying on me?' his stepfather asked.

'I wasn't spying.'

'You were crouched down in the dark. Watching.'

'I was going to the house on the hill.'

His stepfather grunted. Cleared the crackle in his throat. Hawked a foamy, doughy ball that slapped the pavement.

'What for?'

'There's a man there. He's all beaten up.'

'So?'

'So I wanted to check if he was all right.'

'Why?'

James thought about that. And then he said it anyway.

'Because that's what Mum would have done.'

His stepfather looked up into the night sky and growled at the stars. The alcohol made him sway. He rubbed his face with one big hand. Taking out his pack of cigarettes, he lit another and the smoke seemed to calm him.

'So that's where you go off to on your own?'

The cigarette glowed. Smoke blew grey in the dark. His stepfather looked up into the sky again. Jabbed at the heavens with a finger.

'Think she's up there, watching us?'

James shrugged.

'No? You sure?'

James shook his head. No, he wasn't sure at all.

His stepfather smiled, just enough to show the glint of his teeth. 'Means there's bugger all hope for the world if she isn't.' He took a drag on his cigarette then walked a few paces forward and screwed a finger into James's forehead. 'Life goes on for us the way I say it does, because that's how it is now. You and me.' He pushed James backwards, the whole of his weight in the tip of his finger. 'All I'm doing is toughening you up for the world, boy.' He took a final drag and flicked away his cigarette, and it arced like a meteor, and crash-landed and glowed and died.

He looked back at the pub.

And then he looked at James.

His chest crackled gently as he breathed.

'OK,' he said. 'Show me this man of yours.'

The village was silent below them. The odd orange light shimmered. In the distance was Falconbury.

15

Bright. Like a spaceship had set down in the dark of the countryside. James looked out at it from the window, listening to his stepfather walking round the small bedroom in the moonlight, the floorboards creaking with his weight.

And then the man stopped. 'Well?'

James just kept staring out of the window. In the cold night light he could see an angry patch of ground below him, beaten raw. The stick was lying where he had left it. Like a bone picked clean. Suddenly, he wished he had it in his hand.

'You made him up.'

'No,' said James, turning round, 'he was, he—' But James's stepfather raised his hand to shush the boy.

'You made him up because you were spying on me. Spying for her.'

'N—'

And then his stepfather was a ghost scudding through the dim, forcing James back until he was trapped in the jaws of a corner.

'Now apologize.'

James drew a breath. His body shuddered as his stepfather placed a large hand on the wall beside his head and leant in closer. His breath was beery, coarse with tobacco.

'You're a lucky boy. Lucky to be alive. Lucky to have a roof over your head. In fact . . .' He shook as he took a deep breath that broadened his shoulders and neck. 'You got all the luck.'

James could feel his legs wobbling, but he stayed upright, looking straight back. 'You were the one driving,' he replied in a quiet voice.

His stepfather's eyes narrowed. His face flickered. And James knew his stepfather hated him as much as he hated him back, as though a fuse had been lit inside each of them that would never go out. But he knew of nothing in the world that would ever change it.

'You think it's my fault? That I should be apologizing to you?' James's stepfather unbuckled his belt and slid it out from the loops on his jeans. 'I wasn't driving the car that hit us, was I? Don't you go blaming me for what happened, you little shit.' He folded the leather belt in half and then pulled it hard from both ends, making a loud crack. Goosebumps misted over the back of James's neck. 'Now apologize for ruining my evening.'

James shut his eyes. In the black he imagined the man in the greatcoat sitting on the floor, looking up at him. But, when the belt snapped again, James could only picture bright red sparks dancing hot over his skin. He opened his eyes and saw his stepfather wrapping the belt tight round his fist, swaying a little from the beer in his legs. And then he noticed someone else standing in the doorway. It was the man in the greatcoat, holding a green beanie hat, watching everything that was going on.

James gasped.

'There *was* someone here. He's behind you.'

His stepfather grinned. Shook his head.

'Nice try,' he said, flexing his leather-bound fist, then raising it as he began to shout.

But another voice was shouting too.

The man in the greatcoat thundered over the floor towards them.

A stray boot caught James in the knee and he cried out and collapsed into the corner. The floorboards beneath him were as hard as bone.

When he looked up, he saw his stepfather flat against the wall, the sharp edge of an old kitchen knife lying against the soft white pipe of his throat. The man in the greatcoat was holding it, his free arm pinned across the other man's chest. On the floor was the green woollen beanie with raspberries and tiny wild strawberries spilt around it. A handful of hard red cherries rolled like marbles in the moonlight then struck the wall and stopped.

James's stepfather struggled to breathe. Spit whistled in his teeth and white streamers unfurled and stuck to his chin. A leg began to jerk. And the jerkiness spread until his whole body shook.

When the man in the greatcoat let go, James's stepfather tumbled to all fours and stayed there, panting like a dog, looking down at the floor.

'You try to hit that boy again and it'll be the last time. We go hurting children and the world's gone mad. MAD!'

He looked at James. The gash on his cheek had almost healed and he was far stronger than he had been before. But James dared not speak or ask a single question.

'I'll be watching you both. All the way home.' Then he turned to look out of the window and dropped the kitchen knife into the pocket of his greatcoat and waited for them to leave. When they reached the door, he turned back around. 'Bad things happen to good people,' he said to James who paused, hoping for more. But the man in the greatcoat clicked his tongue. Shook his head. 'I'm damned if I can tell you why.'

The two of them walked back down the hill towards the village in silence. The one time James looked back he saw a figure, silhouetted in one of the upstairs windows, watching them as he said he would.

James did not sleep at all. Every creak in the house was his stepfather pacing up and down the landing, back and forth past his bedroom door.

Eventually, he pulled back the curtains so he could see the house on the hill. So the man there might be able to see him too.

The man who had been fine, just like he said he would be.

Who was stumped by the same sort of questions as him.

June 9th

5

The school was in Falconbury. It sucked in kids from the villages scattered outside the town. You could learn what was happening miles away by wandering round the playground at break. It was like turning the dial on a radio.

James was kicking a stone across a hopscotch court, his hands turning sweaty in his pockets, when he heard about the fair on the outskirts of town. Three boys from his year were sitting against the black wire fence, talking, as he walked past.

Everyone knew about the travellers. They came to Falconbury each summer and set up camp. A fairground would blossom on the rough ground just outside the town for a few days and then disappear, leaving snowdrifts of food wrappers and fish-and-chips papers. James used to go with his mum every year. The last time had been the best. He had won a goldfish in a bag by throwing a hoop around it. And an old woman had read his fortune, telling him he would travel the world. He hoped she was right.

James edged a little closer to hear the three boys properly, keeping close to the fence, kicking at a tuft of grass that had grown through the black wire eyes. His stepfather would not allow him to go to the fair. So this was as close as he could get.

'. . . and there I am, in the dark, peeing up the side of this caravan with bright green writing on it, when the door opens. And I'm thinking, *You div.*' One of the boys was telling a story and the other two laughed. 'Because, suddenly, there's two blokes standing on the steps, looking down at me, and one of them's holding a shotgun.'

'And your pecker's out?'

'Yeah. I'm like full stream.'

All three of them laughed.

'Then what?'

'The one with the gun asks if I'd like him peeing up the side of *my* house.' One of the other boys laughed again. 'So I start saying *sorry* and zipping up and walking away all at the same time, trying not to piss myself, when one of them shouts out and asks if I've seen anyone else around the caravans. Because they're looking for somebody.'

'Who?'

'A man. Black hair. Wearing a blue greatcoat, they said.'

'And what did you say?'

'*No*. Because all I'm thinking is, I need to disappear before they shoot me. Or worse. But before I can run I hear the gun clicking and a voice telling me to stand still. And then there's footsteps. And I'm thinking, this is it. I'm dead. Till one of them spins me round and asks if I'm sure I haven't seen the man they're looking for. And I tell him *no* again. But this time he opens up a little bag and drops something into his hand for me to see.'

'What?'

'Gold, mate. A piece of fricking gold. And he tells me if I hear anything about who they're looking for then I could end up getting rich.'

There was a hushed silence in the group until one of them burst out laughing and shook his head.

'It's true, mate. If anyone here knows anything, I'll split it with you.'

'Gold? Really? You're joking.'

James was already walking away when he heard a shout and someone getting up behind him, the wire fence rattling and springing back. But he kept looking ahead, walking straight towards a teacher who was patrolling the playground and teasing a group of kids complaining about their homework.

When a ray of sun drifted over him, he held out his hand, imagining it was gold warming his outstretched palm. He wondered how much he would need to buy every one of his dreams.

6

James wandered up and down the muddy avenues between the caravans, looking for the right one. Somewhere bacon was cooking. He passed a cube of hay bales and walked golden stalks into the mud.

Rounding a corner, he came upon a group of boys not much younger than him, lounging on the grass, their torsos browned in the sun and the whites of their eyes shining back at him. One of them shouted out about his school uniform and the others laughed. When something pinged against his backpack, he disappeared behind a veil of red sheets drying on a line between two caravans. They smelt of the hospital he had stayed in after the accident. The cool of their shade made him shiver as he stood waiting for the laughter to stop.

After taking off his tie and putting it in the front

pocket of his backpack, he walked on with his blazer bunched under his arm.

The fairground was pitched on a patch of waste ground in the distance, quiet and gloomy, like a grounded ship in the daylight. Gulls rose suddenly from the peak of the helter-skelter tower, wailing to each other, as though the silence had spooked them, or perhaps bored them. Suddenly, the fair looked so worn and small that James felt like an old man trying to remember what had been so fascinating about all the whirr and colours and noise.

When he spotted the caravan with bright green lettering on the side and a small set of wooden steps in front of the door, he stopped. Somewhere a dog growled. James saw it. Large and black, lying in the crawl space underneath the caravan, with its ears pricked towards him.

It crept forwards, a thick metal chain uncoiling behind it, its hindquarters swelling as it stood up.

When it growled again, James turned round to leave.

And then he heard a door opening.

'Hey,' said a man's voice behind him. 'Whatchoo want, little man?' The nape of James's neck bristled. He kept staring back the way he had come. 'Whatchoo want, I said?'

The dog barked.

The chain danced and clinked.

James turned back around.

The traveller was standing on the top step. He was wearing a waxy green coat, even though it was warm, and a flat cap was pushed back on his head. Another man was standing with him, peering out from the doorway.

The lie James told them was exactly as he had planned to say it, shot through with glimmers of truth to make it seem more real.

His hands were clenched inside his pockets the whole time.

7

The old brown car smelt of stale beer and the spent butts squashed into the ashtrays his stepfather left lying round the house. The footwell was ankle deep in receipts, newspapers and flyers for the fair. The plastic back of the driver's seat had been slashed diagonally from top to bottom and nuggets of orange sponge had settled everywhere like down.

The two men in the front seats said nothing. The one wearing the green jacket and the flat cap was driving. The other one coughed and spat a foamy, stringy missile through his half-open window before winding it shut. He pulled down the sun visor and inspected his face in the mirror, picking at a spot on his nose. Eventually, he said something to the driver in a language that James did not understand and both men laughed.

When the driver's eyes caught James watching him, the boy looked away. The nugget of gold was still there in his hand when he opened it, shiny with sweat. He had puffed out his chest and demanded it before agreeing to show the travellers where the man in the greatcoat was hiding. They had told him he bargained like a man when it was placed in his outstretched palm, promising him more if they found who they were looking for.

But James knew that, however hard he tried, he was not a man like them. The travellers were brawny with stubbled faces. Great lines of black hair ran down the backs of their fingers. There was a musk about them like woodsmoke.

'Yoo'se gonna be even richer, boy, if we catch him,' said the one in the passenger seat who had turned round to look at James. The driver in the flat cap laughed out loud.

'Long as he's telling us the truth.'

'Course he is,' said the other one and kept staring until James heard the hammer of his heart.

'Course I am,' he said and forced himself to stare straight back.

And the man just nodded.

'Well, don't go spending it all at once now,' he said and smiled. His teeth were rickety stumps, whittled through and browned like rocks suffering the trickle of water.

8

'The barn's beyond the village,' said James, leaning forward. 'You can go round the back road to get there. Take the next left.'

The car took the turning. Both travellers looked up at the house on the hill as they passed it.

'What's that place?' asked the driver.

'The house on the hill. No one ever goes there.'

'Why's that?'

'Too dangerous. It's all falling in.'

The one in the passenger seat shook his head.

'That wouldn't bother our man,' he said and gave it another glance.

'It was definitely the barn,' said James, rolling the piece of gold between his fingers. 'That's where I saw him. Looked like he was making a bed up in the hayloft.' Silt gathered in his throat. It was difficult to swallow.

James knew that lies were better when they were told simply. The driver watched him in the mirror, his eyes flicking back and forth to the road.

'Don't worry, son,' he said eventually. 'We all gotta learn to look after number one. Yer mam and da en't gonna be around forever.'

'Yeah,' said James, nodding. 'I know.' And then he looked down into the footwell and listened to the rumble of the car on the road.

He wondered what his mother would say if she could see him sitting in this car, lying to these men to get their gold. He wasn't sure if there was a place for people who had died. Sometimes he wished there was. But there were other times when he told himself such a place couldn't possibly exist because the stories about it seemed so old and worn through and of a different world entirely.

The barn was shut. Two big black doors, with a metal bar hanging down. The travellers approached the building cautiously, one from the front, the other circling round and approaching from the back. They kept low to the ground, creeping like mist. James watched them, leaning against the old brown car parked down the track near the turning they had taken off the lane.

He knew that they would not find the man in the greatcoat, however hard they looked, amongst the old farm machinery on the lower floor. And, even though there was a ladder up to the hayloft, all they would find upstairs would be grain sacks, some piled as high as the boy's waist, others laid down to make a bed for whenever he lied to his stepfather about 'pretend' friends having invited him to a sleepover.

Sacks.

And a makeshift bed.

Puddles of grain.

And rat droppings.

He stared at the gold in his hand, trying to calculate how much this one piece might be worth. Turning it round in the sunlight, his smile disappeared as it occurred to him how easy lying was. He placed the nugget between his teeth, remembering how the prospectors during the Gold Rush in America had tested their treasure to see how soft and golden it really was.

When he bit down, it was as hard as iron. Fool's gold was what the prospectors had called it.

Inside him, hope turned to dust.

He had lied.

But the travellers had lied too.

He was a fool.

But the travellers were less foolish than him.

They were men and he was just a boy.

When the two of them emerged from the barn, they stood in the sunlight, talking. One of them lit a cigarette. The golden wheat fields surrounding them hissed in the breeze. Eventually, the man stubbed out his cigarette and both of them walked back to the car.

'He could have gone to Hemingsford. That's the next town,' said James, pointing away from Timpston. 'It's not too far. An hour's walk maybe, if you stay on the footpath.'

'Could be,' said the one in the flat cap. And then he held out his hand. A large, callused palm. Deep creases blackened with dirt. 'Change of plan. You come and see us next year instead. We'll let you into the fair for free and throw in a couple of rides. I never forget a face.'

'Yeah,' said James, nodding, 'I will.' And he placed the nugget of make-believe gold into the open palm in front of him. And the man in the flat cap stared at him for what seemed like an age.

The other one coughed.

'Hemingsford, you reckon?'

'Yes,' said James. But the man was not talking to him.

'Nah,' said the other one and dropped the lump of gold back into his drawstring bag and pulled the cords tight.

James was walking back down the dusty track to the lane with his backpack over his shoulder and his blazer under his arm when the car drove past him and a window rolled down.

'Nice working with ya,' one of them shouted and both men laughed.

At the end of the track the old brown car turned left, away from the village. James watched it until it disappeared into the shimmering line of wheat.

And he kept staring for a good while after that.

9

He walked back along the lane towards the village for about a mile before taking a footpath that cut through hazel and waist-high bracken and joined the road winding up around the hill towards the house. Below him, Timpston was hazy in the warm. He picked out his house, a terracotta cube. Nearby, the cross on the church tower flashed golden in the late afternoon sun.

He watched for the old brown car and the travellers, but there was no sign of anybody. So he crept in through the kitchen as he usually did.

He was in the bedroom, sitting on the old green sofa. James knew the man must have heard him walking up the stairs. Seen him on the landing. Yet there he was, still slumped on the cushions. So he smiled. And the man nodded back.

'There's a couple of men from the fair looking for you.'

'How do you know?'

'I heard about them at school.'

'And you thought you should tell me?'

James shrugged and looked down at his black school shoes. His mum had picked them out a week before she died, and now his toes were touching the ends and the tops were scuffed with tiny half-moons.

'I owe you,' he said.

'You do?'

'For last night.'

The man got up from the sofa and looked out of the window, keeping close to the wall, careful not to show himself to anyone who might be outside.

'I told them I saw you in a barn, on the other side of the village.'

But the man kept looking out of the window anyway and only when he seemed to be satisfied that nobody was outside did he turn back round.

'So you've spoken to them then?'

James curled his fingers into fists and then released them. He nodded. But the man was waiting for him to explain.

'They're giving out gold to anyone who can help them find you. Only it's fool's gold.'

'Well,' said the man, laughing lightly in his throat, 'there's a lesson for you. Not everything in this world is what it seems. Not gold. Or men. Or even boys, come to that.' He sat back down on the sofa and wrapped his greatcoat around him. The deep cut on his face was now just an angry scar and James began wondering again how it had healed so quickly.

'What do they want with you?' he asked.

'Nothing. It's a misunderstanding.' And then something occurred to him. 'I wouldn't ever hurt you,' he said sternly.

'I know,' said James in a tiny voice and nodded to make sure the man believed him.

'What were you planning on doing with the gold? If it had been real?'

'Leave. If it was enough.' He dragged the edge of his school shoe backwards and forwards, drawing hazy rubber lines on the wood. 'He's my stepdad.'

'And he crashed the car?'

'Yeah,' said James, remembering what the man must have heard last night. 'Over a year ago.'

'So you blame him for what happened to your mum, and he's angry at being left to look after you?' James said nothing because the man already seemed to have worked everything out. 'There must be someone else. What about your real father?' But James just shook his head. 'Was it always like this?'

James blinked himself steady. 'It was different when Mum was about,' he said.

'Well, I've got some news for you,' said the man, clicking his tongue and looking out of the window at the hills. 'It's not much better out there, unless you find a good spot.'

'How do you find one of those?'

'I'm not sure anyone knows. Or else the ones who do are keeping it a secret.' He pointed a dirty finger at the writing chalked over the black painted wall. 'So what's all this?'

'Ideas. For what I'm going to be.'

'Doctor . . . Lawyer . . . Architect . . . Biologist . . .'

'I'm still working it out.'

The man grinned. Folded his arms. Settled back in the sofa.

'So running away would still mean school then?'

James shrugged. He looked out at the hills and tried not to think too hard about the future.

'There's a lot that isn't on that wall,' said the man.

James let out a long, slow breath. 'No one knows how the world works, do they?'

'No. They don't.'

'Do you think there's someone in control of it all? Making up the rules?'

'If there is, they've got a funny way of going about it.'

The two of them smiled. And the house seemed to broaden and breathe after that.

Sunlight began chasing itself over the floor and the walls. And the man watched it. And James watched the man. And it seemed to be enough for the moment that he was standing there.

'Do you mind if I sit down for a bit?' asked James when their eyes met.

'It's your house.' He made to get up off the sofa, but James waved him back down and sat cross-legged on the floor, leaning against the wall with his backpack and blazer beside him. Then he stood up and picked up the piece of chalk from the window sill and rubbed off the last digit from the number on the black painted wall, changing it from

$$1,641$$

to

$$1,640$$

He put the chalk on the window sill and sat back down on the floor. The man stared at the wall as he dug out a plastic bottle of water from his greatcoat pocket that looked as though it had been refilled dozens of times, and unscrewed the top and took a sip. He shook his head.

'Tell me. I can't figure it out.'

'It's the number of days till I'm eighteen,' said James.

'So that makes you, what? Thirteen . . . and . . .' He twirled his finger around beside his head. 'Thirteen and . . . something now?'

'Yeah.'

The two of them sat opposite each other for a while until James noticed the man's hands were trembling ever so slightly as he held the plastic bottle in his lap and his brow was glistening with sweat. So the boy took an exercise book out of his backpack.

'I've got an essay to write.'

'What's the title?'

James kept staring at the blank page, the biro spinning round his fingertips.

'Why the Hell is the World Like it is?' he said eventually. And both of them laughed.

'What's it really about?'

'Are Blue-green Algae Really Bacteria?' And they both laughed again and the man shook his head, muttering to himself that the world had gone mad.

He sat quietly as James began writing. And, after a while, his hands seemed to settle and his brow no longer shone, and he screwed the top back on the half-empty bottle of water and put it back in his greatcoat pocket.

When James reached the bottom of the page, he looked up and asked the man what he was thinking about, and he replied that he was daydreaming about someone.

'Who?'

'The person I used to be.'

'Everyone changes,' said James. 'People just get older.'

'Yes,' said the man, nodding. 'They do.'

When James looked down at the page again, he found he was unable to write because his hand was frozen.

'What's wrong?'

'Nothing.'

But there was. And James looked back at the wall, wanting to rub out everything that was written there.

'Your mum'll know somehow. She'll be proud of you, whatever you do.'

James looked at him.

'How will she know?' he asked.

But the man could not answer that. So he closed his eyes and listened to the world turning. And, eventually, he heard the boy writing again.

When the sun disappeared over the backs of the hills, the sky flushed even more bloody and pink, and then began to darken. Clouds, stretched thin as bubblegum, broke. The light was too dim for writing any more.

James folded his book shut. Put it in his backpack. Pulled up the zipper.

The man stood up when he did. Brushed himself down. Held out his hand.

'Thank you,' he said.

'What for?' asked James as they shook. But all he got was a smile.

'What's your name?'

'James.'

'I'm Webster.'

James nodded as though approving of the name. And then he stood there in the failing light, following the shape of the hills, until he was ready to speak.

'You'll be leaving, won't you?'

'Yes.'

'Because of the men after you?'

Webster nodded.

James waited. He wanted to say something else, but the words were just out of reach. So he turned and walked towards the door. But, before he reached the landing, he stopped and looked back.

'Thank you too,' he said, realizing it had been a long time since he had sat with someone else and not felt alone either. Webster raised his hand like an Indian chief.

In the dying light he could have been a ghost, waving goodbye for the very last time.

10

James wandered down the road around the hill and clambered over the rotten stile into the field. But, instead of going home through the grass, he kept on following the hedge until he met a footpath he knew would take him into the centre of the village. He knew there'd be no food at home and he started wondering what he might be able to buy at the shop with the few coins he had in his pockets.

He stopped immediately when he recognized the men's voices.

The two travellers were sitting outside the pub, on top of a wooden picnic table, the soles of their black boots planted on the long bench seat. They were talking to James's stepfather. All three of them were drinking pints and smoking.

James stood at the end of the street, hidden behind the corner of a cottage, and watched them darkening in the failing light. He held his breath when the traveller wearing the flat cap drew out the drawstring bag and dropped a piece of gold into his stepfather's outstretched hand.

His stepfather weighed the nugget.

Closed his fist.

Pointed at the house on the hill.

James turned . . .

. . . and ran . . .

. . . his backpack bumping him, his blazer bunched under his arm, until he dumped them in the field and sprinted on as fast as he could towards the stile.

He checked all the rooms in the house. But Webster was gone. James told himself it was the best thing that could have happened, even though he did not want to believe it.

When he heard a sound, he crept to the top of the stairs and peered down through the gaps between the wooden banisters into the hall below. One of the travellers was standing beside the front door. It was almost dark, but James could still see the outline of his face. Boots crunched broken glass and broke the silence, and the other traveller wearing the flat cap appeared with a shotgun. He had come in the back way through the kitchen.

Both of them stood listening for a moment.

And then they began to make for the stairs.

James eased back, keeping his head down, retreating on to the landing.

A shout.

The thump of boots.

And James sucked his soul in tight.

But neither of the men emerged.

When James looked again, he saw Webster standing in the hall, arms raised, his green woollen beanie in one hand, swollen with berries. The traveller in the flat cap was pointing the gun at him. The other one walked towards Webster and tore his woollen hat from him. When he saw the handle of the old kitchen knife sticking out of one of the pockets of the greatcoat, he drew it out and handed it to the man holding the gun who dropped it into a jacket pocket of his own.

'Whatchoo running out on us for?' said the traveller in the flat cap. 'Don't we treat you nice enough? We got a cosy cage waiting for you.'

'You'll have to kill me first,' said Webster.

'We en't gonna do that,' laughed the traveller. 'You can't make us rich if yoo'se dead.' He walked forward and jabbed the butt of the gun into Webster's face, dropping him to his knees.

Blood.

Spit.

And wheeze.

James shuddered as though he had been hit too.

47

'There's a cure,' said Webster in short, wretched breaths. Both travellers laughed. 'It's true.'

'Who told you that? The person who let you out?' The traveller wearing the flat cap muttered something under his breath when Webster said nothing else. 'There's no cure for what you got, my friend. It's the work of the devil. It can't be undone.' And Webster took another hit between his shoulder blades and collapsed to the floor.

'Please,' he gasped. But the travellers ignored him as he lay coughing at their feet, curled up into a question mark beside them.

'Go on and bring the car round, Swanney,' said the one in the flat cap. 'We need to get this one back where he belongs.'

The man called Swanney disappeared out of the front door. The other one kept staring at the floor, the gun aimed at Webster, his back to James who was looking on like an audience member from the balcony seats.

Moonlight silvered the hallway and the stairs as clouds moved and shadows hardened. James could see the top of the traveller's flat cap directly below him, like the solid top of a column he could cat-leap down to. And then, in the next moment, he stood up and reached for the cracked white chamber pot sitting on the sideboard, which was set against the peeling wall.

However hard he tried, he could not forget himself. The heartbeats deep and rich in his ears. The breathing in his chest. And he knew who he was, and what he might yet become, as he leant over the wooden railing, his arms out in front of him, the pot clamped between his hands.

He froze as the traveller man peeled off his cap and wiped his brow with his forearm as if the moonlight was warming him. There was a balding spot on his crown. So white it was pink.

James's heart wavered.

And then he saw Webster staring up at him through the cold light.

The traveller kicked out, catching Webster in the guts, making him gasp.

And James did not close his eyes, he did not look away, as he released the pot and willed it through the air. Weightless. Not a chamber pot any more, its nature changing on its flight and becoming something else entirely.

And then it ceased to be anything at all as it broke over the top of the traveller's head.

11

James crept down the stairs even though the traveller was motionless.

The man's boots were connected at the heels like one black tailfin and in the dark he looked like the silhouette of some sea creature washed ashore. His cap was upturned like a giant oyster shell. There were white pieces of chamber pot scattered all around him on the hard stone floor and the shotgun lay by his side.

Not a sound. Except for the silence.

'Is he dead?' James whispered.

Webster wiped his mouth with the back of his hand. Spat a gob of blood.

'Maybe.'

James began to shake. His chest was gone. The ends of his fingers were drifts of smoke and he felt as though he was starting to float. When he closed his eyes, he

saw his mother staring back at him, shouting something, which he could not hear above the ringing in his
head.

At the sound of a car engine he opened his eyes,
listening to the vehicle drawing closer as it rounded the
road at the top of the hill. When the headlights shone
shadows through the windows, Webster crouched
down, dragging the boy with him, to keep him out of
the light.

A black half-moon was appearing either side of the
traveller's green jacket, around his hips, leaking out of
him like oil. Carefully, Webster lifted the body to look
beneath it. His old kitchen knife had pierced the inside
material of the jacket pocket and lodged in the man's
stomach.

Outside, the car stopped and the engine idled.

'Come on then, Billy,' shouted Swanney.

The traveller on the floor groaned. Shuddered.

Webster jolted back, keeping below the beam of the
headlights. James scrabbled backwards too.

'What's the problem?' shouted Swanney more
urgently. And then a car door opened and clunked shut,
and the engine rattled as it kept on running.

Footsteps picked their way over the rutty tarmac on
the driveway.

The traveller, Billy, groaned again. One of his hands
scrabbled at the flagstone floor as he tried reaching for

the shotgun. When he attempted to shout out, all he could muster was hot air. He turned his head slowly and looked at James.

'I tolllddd yooo,' he wheezed, his top lip curling round like a dog's. 'I neverrr forrrggeettt ahhh faaacce. Nevvverrrr.'

James gasped.

He shivered.

He was not thinking.

And then he was. As though he had been plugged back into the world.

'Come on,' he said to Webster. 'This way.' And he ran quickly towards the kitchen and the back door.

They crept around the side of the house. The old brown car was parked in the large circular driveway, empty of its driver, with dim-lit holes for headlights, the engine purring as it idled.

'Can you drive?' James asked.

Webster nodded and hitched his greatcoat around him. The two of them ran to the car and opened the doors.

A voice rose inside the house. There was a shout.

James slammed the passenger door shut. Webster's hands shook as he worked his feet and tried switching gears, but there was a nasty grating sound and then the engine stalled. He twisted the keys in the ignition, forcing the motor to churn over and over, and James's stomach seemed to shrink, smaller and smaller.

And then the car started.

Webster released the handbrake and worked the pedals and the gears, turning the vehicle around until it was pointing back down the hill. A shout rang out behind them. And then a sound like the crack of a whip flashed in the dark and the wing mirror on James's side of the car exploded with a bang. For a terrible moment he thought he had been shot too.

'Get down,' ordered Webster, who slumped down in his seat, keeping one hand on the steering wheel. There was another gunshot. The back of the car thumped and groaned, and James felt it through his bones.

Moths scattered in the weak beams of the headlights as the car hurled them down and round the hill.

When they reached the bottom, they came to a cross-roads. The engine grumbled and the doors shuddered as the two of them sat staring through the windscreen. James gripped the edges of the seat and pushed himself up until he could see the rooftops of the village just below them silvered by an oval shaped moon. He wondered if this was the last time he would ever see Timpston. It was not how he had imagined his leaving.

Every blink was like a camera clicking.

'You can't come with me.' Webster's blue eyes were burning. His face was stone.

'I can't stay here,' whispered James. 'Not now. They'll find me. Just like they found you.' He thought he heard something and looked round, back into the dark behind them, thinking that someone was there. But all he saw was the house on the hill, up above them, as if floating in the dark.

'I'll always be grateful to you. For helping me. I will. But it's not safe being with me. I'm not like normal people. You heard them. They said it was the work of the devil. That it can't be undone.'

'What can't? I don't understand.'

Webster looked away. His fingers drummed the steering wheel. He sucked in his cheeks and let out a long, slow breath.

'Do you believe in fairy tales?' he asked. James opened his mouth. Then shut it again. And Webster turned to look at him. 'Well, I didn't either. Not until a few weeks ago. Now I believe in all sorts of things.'

'Why? What happened?'

'I was attacked in the night.' Webster squeezed the top of the steering wheel as he remembered. 'I was attacked by something as close to me as you are now. But I still couldn't tell you exactly what it was for sure. It all happened so fast.'

'What did it look like?'

'Like a man but larger, with teeth the length of your fingers. Knives for hands. Eyes the colour of wasps. I tripped. Fell all the way down a bank. When I came round in the morning, I couldn't move for the brambles. I was bloody. Sore. Barely alive. The travellers found me walking down the lane in a state. They helped at first. But when I told them what had happened they locked me up. Told me I was going to make them rich. Because I'd been attacked on the night of a full moon . . .' Webster's voice tailed off.

'By what?' James saw the glitter of questions in his head. His tongue touched the roof of his mouth. 'You mean by a—'

But Webster shushed him, as if he had the power to break the world in half with just a single word, leaving James's heartbeats sounding louder than any statement he had thought of uttering.

'I believe them too,' said Webster, 'because I've seen the travellers do things. Things you'd never imagine were possible.'

'What sort of things?'

But Webster just shook his head and looked away.

James kept on trying to think of the right thing to ask.

'You don't believe me, do you?' Webster squirmed in his seat and pulled back the collar of his greatcoat to reveal two large scars disappearing down the back of his neck, the skin still tender and pink around them. 'You tell me then. What else could have done that?' And James kept staring because he had no answer. And then he remembered how the gash on Webster's face had healed so quickly, wondering how such a thing could have happened to any normal man.

'They told me it'll happen at the next full moon,' said Webster, releasing his collar.

'What will?' whispered James.

'That I'll change.' Webster's breath became shorter. 'Transform.' His fingers attached themselves to the steering wheel, and then he peeled them off and drew his arms tight around him, as though guarding against his body splitting apart there and then. Slumped in the seat, he seemed smaller than James remembered him being before. 'I'm not a bad person. But I'm not the person I used to be either. That's why you can't come with me.'

James thought he heard a sound again, behind the car, and looked round. But there was nobody there. As he stared through the rear window, into the dark, he saw playing out in the void what would happen if he stayed in Timpston, and he looked away. His eyes met Webster's, the two of them staring in silence, until the fear inside James became too much to bear.

'You told them there's a cure. I heard you.'

Webster nodded.

'An old traveller broke me out of the cage I was in. He told me I should pray to God. Ask to be led to one of his saints. St Hubert. Because he said that way I might find a cure, a key I could use to banish evil.' He shrugged and blew out a long, slow breath. 'That's it. That's all there is.'

'Don't you believe in God?'

Webster sighed. He dropped his head back and looked up.

'Do you?'

They sat there not speaking for what seemed like an age, with the dark pressing all around them, and the car engine rumbling. And James began wondering if Webster was scared too, but couldn't say it out loud because the world of men was not built that way. When he saw the moon reappearing from out of the cloud, he cleared his throat and spoke.

'How long until the next full moon?'

'A week, I think.'

'Then I'll help you try and find a cure before then.'

Webster sat up purposefully in his seat. His fingers gripped the steering wheel tight. And then he sat perfectly still for a moment.

'So you believe what the travellers told me too?'

James nodded. 'Because we can't not, can we? At least not until the next full moon.'

And Webster looked at him for a moment and then shook his head.

'No,' he said, 'we can't.' He sighed and looked down at his knees. 'Are you sure you want to leave? With me?'

'Yes.'

'Because of your stepfather?'

'Because of everything.'

Webster said nothing else for a while and James gripped the seat, steeling himself for what he was going to say next if the man said *no*.

'What if we don't?' asked Webster finally.

'Don't what?'

'Don't find a cure in time.'

'Then it's not meant to be. None of it.'

'And if we do?'

'Then it is. And we'll decide what to do after that.'

Webster sat listening to the car engine.

'OK,' he said. 'A week. A week and we'll see if anything good comes of it. Because no one knows the future, do they?'

'No,' said James. 'No one knows how the world works at all.'

And Webster nodded and let off the handbrake, and put the car into gear and turned the steering wheel, and Timpston slid slowly out of sight.

The rear lights of the car glowed like the ends of cigarettes and eventually vanished into the dark.

Up on the hill, a figure emerged from the house. It was Swanney. The shotgun was crooked over his arm and the smell of gunpowder was still ripe in the air. He was speaking quickly on a mobile phone.

June 10th

12

James clicked the link to print. Somewhere near the front of the Internet café a printer warmed and whirred, and he followed the *click-clack* sound of the pages until he was standing over them.

The warm paper smelt of bleach.

He paid for ten sheets of A4 and folded them over to fit more easily into his hand. Two pounds for the printing and a pound for an hour on the Internet didn't seem too much at all for finding out what they wanted to know.

And it was easier than asking God.

During the night, James had secretly tried praying to find out more about St Hubert. And Webster had admitted to doing the same. But neither of them knew if their questions had even been heard. And then James had thought of using the Internet.

He sat on a bench outside the café and made notes in the margins of the pages, periodically looking up to see if Webster had returned to the car parked across the road. By the time he looked up to see the man standing waving at him, James had read everything through. He narrowed his eyes until Webster was just a man trying to attract his attention.

A man who could be anyone he wanted.

'There's a few cures mentioned,' said James as he sat beside Webster in the car, looking through the pages. 'Wolfsbane. Exorcism. There's even one about addressing somebody three times by their Christian name.' Looking up, he smiled. But Webster didn't seem to notice as he sipped from the old plastic bottle of water he'd taken from his greatcoat pocket.

'What about the one we're after? St Hubert.'

'That's here too.' James ran his finger across a block of text. 'St Hubert is the patron saint of hunters. His key was supposed to be a cure for rabies. It was a metal bar or nail with a decorative head. Priests would heat up the key and place it on the wound to cauterize and sterilize it.'

'My wounds have all healed up. You've seen the scars.'

James looked up from his pages again.

'An old traveller woman worked on them,' explained Webster. 'Open and red the first day, closed the next.

She used an ointment which I was supposed to keep rubbing on.' He stood the bottle of water in the well between them and dug out a small glass pot from a trouser pocket and twisted off the black plastic top. Spots of granular yellow paste were dried out around the rim. James smelt hints of beeswax and sugar and olive oil. 'It worked for my face too,' said Webster, running a finger down the scar on his cheek. 'I caught it on a fence in the dark after I escaped from them.'

James studied the scar on the man's face as though still unable to believe it. And then he smoothed down the fold in the pages, making them crackle.

'It says here the key was used for other reasons too. To cure all sorts of evil,' he said, sifting through the pages until he found what he was looking for. 'The nearest church dedicated to St Hubert is in Dorset. I printed out directions. It's a couple of hours according to Google.'

'A church? I haven't been to one of those in a while.'

'Neither have I. Not since I went with Mum. We used to go most Sundays. She said it made a difference.'

'Did it?'

When James didn't answer, Webster screwed the cap back on the bottle of water, and put it in his greatcoat pocket along with the ointment, and gripped the steering wheel. 'Your seat belt,' he said as he turned the key in the ignition and pushed up the indicator to turn out on to the road. James reached round for the belt and dragged it down and clicked the metal head into the plastic socket below his hip. He ran a hand up and down the line of grey webbing across his chest.

'Do you think he'll be glad to see us?'

'Who?'

'You know.' James jabbed a finger at the ceiling of the car. 'It's a church after all.'

Webster thought about that for a while as they trundled up the road and then he turned and looked at the boy.

'As long as you haven't done anything to piss him off,' he said and smiled. But James did not smile back. He bunched up his shoulders then dropped them down as he sighed so it seemed to Webster that he was melting into nothing.

'He pissed me off first,' James said.

Webster nodded. He listened to the car wheels grumbling in the springs of his seat.

'Yeah. I guess he did.'

They kept to the minor roads. Sometimes the hedges running beside them opened up and they could see great expanses of fields blocked out in different colours and shapes, rising and falling according to the land. Pylons ran empty tramlines in the blue. Telegraph poles broke the horizon at intervals like staples punched by some giant hand to prevent the earth and the sky from breaking apart. James touched the scar beneath his hairline, which was all that was left of the accident, and it was like pressing a button that fired up thoughts in his head. He tried not to think what his mother would say about him sitting in another car, in another time, having left Timpston far behind.

Webster was still nervous about the travellers. Occasionally, he would pull the car into a lay-by and turn off the engine and wait, scrutinizing any vehicle that passed them. James had given up asking him how the men would know where they were.

Eventually, they stopped for petrol. A small garage on the edge of a village with three white pumps the size of refrigerators in the forecourt and potholes in the asphalt, full of black rainwater.

Inside, the grey linoleum floor was scuffed with years of footsteps. Paperbacks with sun-bleached spines were racked in a wire tower that squeaked when it turned. The man behind the counter watched James and Webster as they picked out cans of Coke and a loaf of bread and a packet of rolled pink slices of ham.

Webster paid, peeling off a note from a wad he kept in his trouser pocket. James had no idea where the money was from. And it never seemed the right time to ask.

The man behind the counter wore half-moon glasses on a chain. He tapped the keys hunt-and-peck style on the old plastic till and each number appeared in digital green on the narrow screen. His face was lean and lined, the colour of an estuary at low tide. Black strands of hair were combed crossways over the white dome of his head.

'Nice tat,' said Webster suddenly, nodding at the inside of the man's wrist. James tipped forward and saw the beginning of a word in black gothic script. The man pulled up his shirtsleeve to the elbow for him to see.

Utrinque Paratus

'See much action?' asked Webster.

As the man picked out the right change from the till, he rapped his right thigh with a knuckle and there was a hollow, hard sound as though he was knocking on a door.

'You?' he asked.

'Yeah,' replied Webster. 'You could say that.'

'And now here we are,' he said, handing Webster his change. 'Here we bloody are. At least you got your boy.' He smiled at James.

'Yes,' said Webster. 'I'm glad to have him.'

'You gonna be a para too, son? Like your dad?' James shrugged. 'No? Well, I don't blame you. Stripping down your SA80 ain't much use out here in the real world.' The man cocked a finger at Webster and pulled the trigger. '*Ready for Anything.* Anything but Civvy Street, right?'

'Ready for anything but life,' replied Webster and the man cackled a laugh that flopped strands of black hair down over his forehead.

As they drove away, James looked back at the garage. The man was hobbling across the forecourt, pulling up a wire chain until it was hanging between four metal posts. Eventually, he disappeared from view as the road bent round.

'Ready for anything,' said James. 'Is that what the Latin said?' Webster nodded. 'Is that what they teach you in the army?' Webster nodded again. 'Isn't it impossible? To be prepared for everything, I mean.'

'Yes,' said Webster. 'But you have to try.'

13

The church was on the outskirts of the town, hidden from the main road by a screen of chestnut trees. Webster parked the car in a side street lined with red-brick houses set back from the pavement, each one an echo of the one beside it. When James opened his door, he smelt newly-cut grass. Diesel. Dirt in the drains.

The afternoon was starting to lengthen and they walked through shadows that crept from walls and corners like outriders of the night. Kids buzzed around the street, screaming and shouting.

When Webster noticed a little girl clip-clopping towards them in red high heels and wearing a set of black beads, he stepped off the pavement and waved her by with a low bow. She was pushing a buggy, its four orange wheels crackling like pepper grinders. A naked plastic baby was strapped in the seat, sitting with its arms outstretched.

After walking past them, the girl wheeled the buggy around and started back down the path, shushing and cooing as she went.

'She won't settle,' she said, going past again.

'She will,' said Webster and grinned at James.

But she shook her head. Pointed at the other kids playing. 'Not with all that noise,' she sighed.

Webster watched her tottering in the heels until he heard something that made him start. When James looked up, he realized the kids playing in the street were shooting each other with imaginary guns. Lobbing imaginary grenades. Dying horribly and eagerly in their made-up world. Webster took a deep breath and started walking, plunging shaking hands into his pockets.

James trailed behind. When they stopped to cross the road, he stepped up beside Webster. 'Did you ever fight in a war?' he asked.

'Yeah.'

'Which one?'

'Iraq.'

James cleared his throat as the man checked for traffic. He lined up his toes on the edge of the kerb and waited until his shoes were perfectly matched.

'Did you ever kill anybody?'

Webster said nothing. A car passed. They stood there for a moment longer and then they crossed the road in silence.

James kept behind Webster the rest of the way, cursing himself.

The church was locked. The large oak door was arched and silvered and ancient, and quartered into four sections by two thin pieces of brown metal, one laid across the other in the shape of a cross.

They walked around the building and tried another smaller door. But that was locked too.

'We'll get in tomorrow,' said Webster as they came back round to the main oak door. James gave him a look. 'Sunday. They must be open on a Sunday, unless the rules have changed.' And he tapped at the service sheet pinned to the cork board in the porch.

James just nodded.

Sunday?

The past couple of days seemed to have passed outside of ordinary time. As though he had dreamt them. He was supposed to have double maths on Monday morning. There was going to be an algebra test.

'You all right?' Webster was staring at him.

'Yeah,' said James. 'I'm good.'

'Well, all right then.' And both of them smiled.

*   *   *

The plastic tables in the café were white. The floor was like a giant-sized chessboard and James tried plotting moves in his mind, with imaginary pieces as big as him, while chewing his burger and dipping his fries in ketchup. But, after one night sleeping in the car, he found it hard to concentrate, as though somewhere inside a valve was gradually tightening. When he started watching other people, laughing and talking, he suddenly became aware of his skin feeling dirty and how much his school shirt and trousers smelt of the travellers' car. As he blinked, gravel seemed to churn at the backs of his eyes.

'Where are we going to sleep tonight?' he asked.

Webster took a slurp of tea.

'We'll get a room. With proper beds. We can't spend another night in the car. I've got enough money.'

James sucked on his Coke. 'Where's it all from?' he asked, trying not to sound too interested.

'The old boy who helped me. He gave it to me. After he let me out of the cage.'

'Why did he do that?'

'Because he wanted to help.'

'Why?'

'I don't know.'

James wasn't sure what to think about that. And he tried not to think too hard about what might happen when the money ran out.

'Thanks for the burger,' he said and rubbed at his tired eyes with a knuckle.

'You saved my life. Remember? That's a whole lot of burgers in my book.' And Webster grinned.

'You saved me first,' said James, wiping his mouth clean with a paper napkin and crushing it into a ball. 'Maybe that's how it's supposed to work.'

'How do you mean?'

'One good thing leads to another.'

Webster clicked his fingers. Smiled.

'You've cracked it,' he said. 'The answer to life.' And, with his mug of tea, he toasted James who beamed because Webster seemed genuinely happy, as if a weight had been lifted from somewhere deep inside. For a moment, the future didn't seem to matter at all.

They sat in silence for some time, watching the street through the freckled, grimy windows, full and content with the world. And then James noticed that Webster was looking carefully at anyone who walked past. Following them down the street.

'You think they'll find us, don't you?'

Webster nodded.

'I don't see how.'

'They will.'

'We'll find the key first,' said James.

'I hope so.' But he kept staring at the world outside.

*   *   *

72

The two of them walked side by side along the pavement like father and son. They stopped outside the window of a charity shop when Webster pointed at a mannequin dressed in a black two-piece suit.

'You'd look good in that,' he said. 'Sharp.'

James swallowed down something stuck in the back of his throat. It might have been a hair. Or grease from the fries.

'I've only worn a suit once,' he managed to say before clearing his throat again. And Webster's smile wavered slightly as he nodded.

James looked the mannequin up and down. When he half closed his eyes, the figure looked like a normal person that could have been him.

They heard a bolt slide across the door. An old woman was locking up the shop.

'Well?' asked Webster. 'Do you want to try it on?'

James looked up into Webster's smiling face and something melted inside him, so he nodded, and Webster ran to the door and banged on it and flapped his wad of notes against the glass.

'The suit!' he shouted. 'We need that suit!'

And both of them laughed as the old woman's flustered face broke into a smile.

James tried it on with a clean white shirt and a tie.

'Looks good,' said Webster.

'Looks sharp,' said James and he struck a pose that made Webster roar.

They chose an armful of jeans and shirts and tops which they stuffed into a duffel bag with worn leather handles that cost less than a pound.

When the old woman let them out of the shop, James told a joke that made her laugh. And he saw in her eyes that she was glad for both of them in some way and it lit a light in his chest, which glowed for some time afterwards.

14

The motel room was a twin. It was cheap and beige. The single dirty window had plastic venetian blinds that worked by pulling on a beaded metal chain like the one in the bath for the plug.

Webster lay on his bed and James on his. The black suit was draped over the back of a chair together with the shirt and tie.

The boy reread the pages he had printed off the Internet, underlining sections here and there that interested him.

'Did he say anything else about St Hubert? Or the key?' he asked Webster.

'Who?'

'The old traveller who helped you escape. The one who gave you the money.'

'No.'

James drummed his fingers on the pages.

'What was he like?'

'Nice enough,' said Webster, staring at the ceiling, his arms in triangles behind his head. 'Sad though. He had a big scar on his face. Like someone had opened him up and pulled out the happiness and stitched him up again.'

'Why do you think he was so sad?'

'His three children hadn't stayed. And he lost his wife a couple of years ago. He loved her very much.'

'How do you know?'

'Because of the way he talked about her. She had golden blonde hair and blue eyes and lips as red as holly berries. She ran away to be with him when she was only sixteen. He gave her a bouquet of daisies on their wedding day because it was all they could afford.'

James stared at Webster, remembering how the woman in the charity shop had smiled at them and how it had made him glow. Suddenly, he wanted to know if Webster had a family too. Anyone. But somehow he didn't want to ask. Not now. Not ever.

When he realised Webster was staring back, he cleared his throat and folded his arms.

'Is that why he helped you?'

'What do you mean?'

'The old man, did he help you to feel better? To stop feeling sad?'

'Maybe.'

'What was his name?'

'Gudgeon.' Webster let out a long, slow breath. 'His name was Gudgeon.'

James wrote down the name in the margin of his notes because he liked the solid, round sound of it. 'Gud-geon,' he said, reading it back. 'And all he told you was to pray to God to find St Hubert's key.'

'Yes.' Webster scratched his face. Banged his head down into his pillow to soften it and laid his arms over his chest. 'I think he helped because he wanted to know if there's really something . . .' James was looking at him. 'You know. Up there?' And he raised his eyebrows at the ceiling. 'Some sort of explanation for it all.'

Neither of them said anything for a while after that. And James began doodling in the margins and gradually a face appeared. An old man. With a beard and long, flowing hair. James worked hard on it for some time, but he could not decide if the drawing was right or wrong or good or bad. He had no idea how to draw the person he was thinking about. Or even if he existed at all. He wrote a name beside it. All three letters of it.

When he woke, it was still dark. The lights in the car park made the blinds soft and yellow around their edges.

Webster was muttering in his sleep. The night before in the car had been the same. He had dreamt loudly, with his head lolled back in the driver's seat and the greatcoat wrapped round him. But now it seemed worse with the bedsheets tight across him. As though it was an illness that had seeped to the surface. Legs kicked. Mattress springs creaked as he moved. His head flashed from side to side over the pillow. James wondered if Webster was dreaming about the night he had been attacked. He was unsure whether to wake him up or not.

Suddenly, the muttering stopped.

Webster rolled over. He opened his eyes and stared straight at James, the blue around his pupils more electric than ever before, the black of his hair richer than a thundercloud. James cried out, afraid. But Webster did not flinch. His face was earnest.

'I killed a little girl in Iraq. All I did was give her a bottle of water because it was so hot. And they hung her up in a tree. To teach everyone else in the village a lesson, so nobody would speak to our unit. All for a bottle of water.'

In the immediate silence they lay staring at each other, across the gap between their beds. And James sensed that the space beside him was as deep as a canyon and he was too afraid to move. Or even speak.

And then Webster shut his eyes and rolled over to face the wall.

James's heart beat into the mattress and the frame of the bed as he lay perfectly still. Heat drifted off his cheeks and his brow, and his hands were curled into fists. He had said nothing to Webster. Nothing at all.

He turned over on to his side and stared into the dirty beige stripes on the wallpaper and listened to the patter of rain starting up against the window, telling himself that Webster had been dreaming. That all this now was a dream of his own making too. But, the moment he closed his eyes, he knew he was not dreaming, he was wide awake, and it broke him out into a sweat that chilled him.

His mind ticked hard.

In the dark behind his eyes he saw the face of a dead girl in a faraway dusty land. And, as he tried to push her back into the dark, the girl became someone. A little younger than him. Brown-skinned. Wearing a grubby, loose dress with blue flip-flops. Bright half-moons on her toenails. A thin silver bangle round her ankle. She was dangling from the branch of a tree. Drifting like a wind chime. An empty plastic bottle lay beneath her on the dusty orange ground, its blue top spun off, a dark wet patch showing where the water had seeped away. Men and women were staring. Wailing. Weeping more tears than would ever fit into that bottle.

Like an item on the six o'clock news.

James opened his eyes and drew up the covers around him, and stared at the wall for a long time, listening to

Webster. The man's breathing gave nothing away. It rolled like a river right through him. James could not be sure if he was awake or not. Whether he might be waiting for him to say something. Finally, he rolled on to his back and stared at the ceiling.

'Sometimes,' he said quietly, 'I speak to my mum. And I tell her things I would never have told her when she was alive. And I don't know what to think about that. And then I just tell myself she probably knows everything now anyway.'

Webster said nothing.

His breathing kept to its same rhythm.

The man did not even stir.

June 11th

15

When James woke up, he sensed he had overslept by the bloated feeling in his head. He panicked for a moment, unsure of where he was. The sensation passed when he saw Webster, showered and dressed, appearing from the bathroom, towelling down his head to leave spikes of black hair.

'Morning,' he said.

'Morning,' said James. 'How did you sleep?'

But Webster didn't seem to hear with the towel buzzing his hair.

The suit smelt clean and soapy and was glassy in spots. The white shirt and tie fitted well. James smoothed down his hair and in the mirror he saw the glimmer of a future where he was grown up, with a job and a house and a family of his own, although he was unsure how he would ever get there.

'Life is everything you want to make of it,' said Webster, as if reading his mind.

And James's heart gleamed because he hoped it was true. But the longer he stared into the mirror, the more he felt something black unwinding through his guts. And the black was cold.

'What's the matter?' asked Webster softly.

But James just shook his head. 'Nothing. I'm OK. Let's go.'

The church was open. An organ was playing as Webster and James crunched along the gravel path between the gravestones. The boy picked at the threads around the buttons of his suit as a shiver licked goosebumps over his skin. That black was in his guts again.

When he looked up, Webster was staring at him. James realized he was standing quite still on the path with his fists clenched.

'I'm fine,' he said, opening his hands.

But then he licked his lips.

Folded his arms.

Shivered in the sunlight and shook his head.

'I'm not as brave as I thought I was.'

Webster bent down beside him. 'I thought the suit might make a good impression,' he said quietly. 'That it was a good idea. I didn't think hard enough about it. I'm sorry. And I'm sorry about your mum too.'

'That's OK. It's not your fault.'

'Think you'll be all right?'

'Yes. I think so. Just give me a moment.'

'Nobody lives forever,' said Webster.

'Why?' asked James in a tiny, cracked voice.

And Webster sighed and shook his head and looked at the gravestones. Some of them lying face down on the grass. Others slowly falling.

James wiped his eyes. Shuddered as he sucked up a breath. 'It's not fair.'

'No. It's not. Whoever decided it must have been as mad as a hatter.'

James managed a smile at that.

Webster crouched down and took hold of the boy's wrists as though they were made of glass. 'I bet your mum's listening to everything you tell her. Wherever she is. So never give up on telling her things.'

And then James bit his lip because he realized what Webster was really trying to tell him. That he had been awake last night.

'I don't have anyone else,' said Webster.

'Neither do I,' James said quickly and squeezed Webster's hands as hard as he could. When the man squeezed gently back, something prickly in James's chest vanished and he breathed more easily after that.

They stayed in the sun, warming themselves, looking into the open black mouth of the church as the organ played. When James stopped shaking, Webster let go of his hands. And when they were ready they went on down the path.

Inside the church, the air was cool, bitter with polish. The stained-glass windows down one side glowed as sunlight played over the flagstone floor. An old man in a dark suit handed both of them a prayer book and a green hymn book as soon as they walked in.

'Feel free to sit wherever you can,' he said, raising his eyebrows because the church was empty except for two old ladies in the front pew.

As Webster and James sat and listened to the music, a handful of other people arrived in ones and twos and took their places.

The service took less than an hour. Webster sang the hymns as loudly as he could, chest puffed out like a pigeon.

James remembered the rhythm of everything as they stood and sat and knelt, just as he had done it with his mother. When he listened to the reading, he closed his eyes to see the story of what was being told. He knelt for communion beside Webster and offered out his hands. In his cupped palms he received a round paper wafer which tasted of nothing except stale air. The sip of wine that followed ran hot into his chest.

Whenever he felt the black in his guts, he worked harder at following the service properly, hoping it might make a difference. And when that didn't work he looked around the church, searching for any clues about St Hubert or the key.

Finally, when the service was over, the organ began to wheeze and play. The two old women at the front rose and shuffled down the nave, drifting like ghosts, their arms locked together as though letting go might mean the end for both of them.

Webster gripped James by the shoulder. He could feel the man's heart beating.

'What do you think? Seen anything that might be important?' James shook his head. Webster pursed his lips and sat back, looking up at the vaulted ceiling. Then he leant in close to the boy. 'Maybe we didn't pray hard enough,' he said before settling back in the pew.

James looked around again for anything that might be helpful and noticed the young vicar talking to a middle-aged couple near the entrance. All three of them were laughing. When the vicar glanced directly at him, James looked away, embarrassed to be caught staring.

'We'll have to ask if we want to find out anything,' he whispered.

When everyone else had left, they approached the vestry and peered at the vicar through a crack in the door. He had already changed out of his robes and was dressed in a black shirt and trousers with a white dog collar around his throat.

'Hello there,' he said when he opened the door and saw them waiting.

'Good morning, Reverend,' said Webster and put out his hand. James noticed that it was shaking. The vicar smiled as he shook it.

'Thank you for coming to the service. And for your marvellous singing.'

Webster beamed. When the vicar looked at James, he suddenly remembered Webster had bought him the suit to help make a good impression.

'I'm James,' he said and held out his hand as Webster had done, making sure it was steady.

'Lovely to meet you, James.' And, for a moment, there was nothing but grace as the vicar smiled, and the pews ticked, and the sunlight moved noiselessly over the stone walls.

Webster wiped his brow with the back of his hand, making it shine.

'We were wondering about the key,' he said quietly.

The young vicar looked taken aback for a moment. And then his face became ashen. James grinned all the harder to try and make up for it. But the vicar looked down at the flagstone floor and shuffled his feet. He planted his hands in his trouser pockets and then straightened up.

'I don't have the key to the donations box,' he said. 'I'm sorry. It can't be opened.'

Webster shook his head. Licked his lips. Patted one of the vicar's shoulders. 'We're not here to take any money. We're not looking to piss you off. That's the last thing we want to do.'

'Oh,' replied the vicar. His forehead creased. His eyes narrowed. 'I'm sorry, I don't—'

'St Hubert's key is what we want to know about,' said James.

'I need to be cured,' said Webster. 'Cured of evil.'

'I see.'

But James knew the vicar did not understand so he took the printed pages out of the inside pocket of his jacket.

'St Hubert's key,' he said, holding up a picture of it. 'It was used as a cure for rabies, but we were told it might also help with other things . . . evil things.'

'And who told you that?'

But neither of them said a word.

'I see. Well, I'm sorry to disappoint you, but there's no key here. I'm not sure there ever has been. That sort of artefact is very rare. A museum piece. Like the one in your picture.'

Webster planted a hand on James's shoulder, squeezing hard, as if to stop himself from falling.

'What if we made a devotion to St Hubert?' asked

James, eyes racing across the text he had highlighted and starred in the margin.

The young vicar folded his hands together in a ball of graceful fingers. His smile was small, but warm and wise.

'What sort of dark and evil things do you need to be cured of?'

'I've been done wrong,' said Webster. 'Someone's done me a great wrong. And now I'm dark inside because of it. I'm something else. Broken apart then put back together.' He wiped his hands over his greatcoat and placed them in his pockets. And then he took them out again and wiped them again. And then he folded his arms tight across his chest, unsure how to stand.

The vicar nodded. As if everything was suddenly clear to him.

'The best and the simplest way to defeat dark and evil things is through love,' he said.

'Love? Who am I supposed to love?' asked Webster.

'Whoever has done you this wrong. It sounds simple, but it's not easy. It's the best advice I can give you.'

'What about asking God?' asked James. 'Could you do that? For us? Just to be sure.'

The vicar pressed his hands together harder and squeezed his lips white, and James thought he might be about to pray. But then he peeled his palms apart and just smiled. Bigger than before. His lips pumping themselves pink again. 'There's no need for that. You'll find out for yourselves that it's true.'

They walked back up the path through the gravestones, crunching gravel. Webster kicked out hard, sending stones skittering into the grass.

'What the hell does he mean?' he asked in an angry voice. 'What do we do now?' He stopped and stared down at his feet then threw back his head and blew out a long breath.

'I think he means you have to forgive whoever attacked you.' James looked through his sheets of paper until he found what he was looking for. 'According to most legends, and what the travellers told you, if someone is attacked on the night of a full moon and survives then they're cursed just like the one who attacks them.'

'So?'

'So, if the vicar's right, you need to find the person who left you cursed and forgive them. They must be out there somewhere.'

'And that'll work? I'll be cured?'

'I don't know. Maybe.'

'A vicar like that wouldn't lie, I suppose.' Webster kicked out at the gravel again. 'It's all shot to shit then. Everything happened like that.' He slapped his palms together with a bang. 'I don't remember anything.'

'Can you remember the place where it happened?'

'Yeah.'

'Then we'll have to start there,' said James. 'See if that helps.'

Webster looked up at the sky. Cupped his hands round his mouth.

'Hey!' he shouted at the blue and the clouds hanging in it. 'Up there! Is this what we're supposed to do? Is this all part of the plan? Well, is it?'

The sun beat down.

Birds flickered and hopped.

The trees hissed as a warm breeze blew.

And it was all they heard.

James took Webster's shaking hands in his and held them until they were steady.

Only then did they walk on down the path.

16

Billy unlocked the steel door of the wagon and glared into the empty corners, just as he had done on the day Webster had vanished. And then he spat into the dirty, brittle straw that covered the wooden floor.

He had checked the boards under his feet and not one of them was loose. All the black iron bars along the front were intact. And the panels on the back wall and at either end were made of hard, solid oak. The ceiling was a flat bed of steel. The only way Webster could have escaped was if someone had let him out.

He turned round when he heard her walking over the grass towards the wagon, the charms and amulets clinking inside the small leather pouch strung around her neck.

'Airght?'

'Airght, Ma,' replied Billy. Her silver hair was scraped back into a bun. Looped over one shoulder was a red leather bag.

She wrapped her black shawl tight around her and walked up the four wooden steps into the wagon, her black shoes clipping and clopping.

'You should've told me sooner about him leaving.'

'I didn't want to worry ya.'

'That right?' Billy heard his blood swelling in his cheeks as she looked at him with a grey half-moon of a smile. She tugged on a couple of the iron bars. 'He en't made of air too, is he?'

'No, Ma,' he said, rolling his eyes. 'Someone let him out.'

'I seen it happen. There was a man once, me and yer da saw him. Vanished in front of our eyes he did. Old magic that was.' She stared through the bars at something Billy could not see.

The chug of machinery working in the distance swept past them on the wind, and Billy glanced towards the patch of waste ground where the fair was being dismantled and packed away for the next town.

'You need anything else, Ma?'

The old woman said nothing as she delved into her red bag and drew out a marionette minus its strings. A wooden man in a dark suit. As tall as her knees until she sat him carefully on the straw. He was wearing small brown brogues with scratched-up soles. And his eyes were nothing more than paint. But he seemed to see Billy all the same.

'Give me what you have then.'

Billy drew out Webster's green beanie hat and the old kitchen knife from his pockets.

'These were his. And his bowl's over there in the corner,' he said, pointing. The old woman took the woollen hat, but shook her head at the knife.

'That won't work,' she said and then shuffled towards the bowl. She picked it up and the puddle of cold broth inside broke its skin as she rotated the bowl in her long, bony hands, her nails tapping on the wood.

'You sure he used this one?'

'Yes.'

The old woman laid down the bowl in front of the marionette and placed the hat next to it. Then she sat down cross-legged in the straw, opposite the wooden figure, like an overgrown child.

When the muttering started, Billy walked back down the steps and stood beside the wagon on the grass. He did not like seeing the darker side of his mother. Her wild eyes. The lips curled back from the gums. Whenever the darkness filled her up, the woman he knew and loved was gone. Like the living dead, he often thought.

Her muttering rippled back and forth.

Wooden joints creaked.

Wooden shoes tapped the floor.

Billy walked further away and lit a cigarette. Out of the corner of his eye, he thought he saw the marionette standing beside his mother, holding her hand. He heard her asking questions. Soft and gentle. The way she used to be with him when he was a boy.

'Billy,' she shouted suddenly, making him jump and almost lose his cigarette. 'You said there was a young lad with him?'

'That's right, Ma. Little sod.'

His mother laughed. The lump on the crown of Billy's head seemed to swell again. He remembered nothing about being knocked to the floor. But James's face haunted him. Lifting up his shirt, he looked at the scar in his side, puckered like an old man's lips now his ma had healed the wound. He rubbed it thoughtfully with his fingers as he pulled long and hard on his cigarette.

'You'll get your chance, Billy,' she shouted. 'We'll find them for you.' And her voice tailed off as she returned to her mutterings. Billy tried to let the sun warm him, but inside he was cold and vengeful. Thinking about the boy. And Webster. And the person who must have freed him from the wagon to set all of this in motion. That was how life worked, it seemed, unfurling from one episode to another, always moving. Like ripples on the surface of a pond.

'Don't forget about who set him free, Ma,' shouted Billy. 'I want their guts for garters 'n' all.' And he took the kitchen knife from his pocket, spun it up and caught it by the handle, and hurled it into the grass, where it stuck.

When it was over and the old woman had packed away the marionette into her red leather bag, Billy returned to the wagon. His mother looked older. Her lips were dry. Her eyes watery and dull, with the skin below them bumpy and mottled like the back of a toad. It was always the same after she had worked with magic. He wondered what deal she had struck with it and what price she might pay for it when she died. But she had never seemed bothered by such thoughts.

She put out her hand and held his arm as he walked her down the steps. He stood with her in the sunlight, wondering when her time would come and whether it would change him.

'I've got a while yet,' she said absently, without bothering to look at him. 'And I en't scared of the beyond neither. For there's nothing there.'

'It don't matter what we do then, does it?'

'The way I see it, it matters all the more,' she said and stared at her son. 'You seen 'em yet? Smelt 'em?'

'What?'

His mother pointed a bony finger at the grass beneath the wagon steps and Billy scanned the fringe of uncut green. When he saw the white tips of them, he went over and knelt down, and picked one up and rolled it in his fingers.

'Turkish,' he said.

'Turkish,' repeated the woman. Billy sniffed the cigarette butt again.

'Smithy grows his own baccy, don't he?'

'Smithy does. He grows his Black Sea Basma. Couldn't grow his own brain bigger than a walnut though.' And the old woman laughed.

Billy smelt the hand-rolled butt again, just to be sure. And then he stared at the ground and imagined how it must have happened. Smithy standing there, making friends with Webster when nobody was watching. Smithy with glue for brains, but fingers like feathers that tickled locks for fun. A gift. Of sorts. A makeweight for everything else that was wrong in his head.

'You don't need magic to see it, do you?' she asked.

Billy shook his head.

'No, Ma,' he said, 'you're right, I don't.' He rubbed his face over with a rough, worn hand. His mother was still staring at him when he looked up. 'I'll go see Smithy. Sort him out.'

'You will,' she said, nodding.

Back in her caravan, she sat by the window and sipped a cup of spicy black tea. The road atlas that belonged to

Billy was not to her liking because it was too old. So she sent him to borrow one that showed the most recent changes to the roads.

When he laid it in front of her on the table, she flicked through it, stopping at each page she needed. She ran a red pen along the route she knew Webster and the boy would be taking, circling the towns they would pass through, and giving a time for their arrival at each one.

'And you're sure.'

'Sure as sure can be.'

Billy held out his palms to his mother.

'Will things work out all right?'

'Ah,' she said, taking his hands by the wrists, 'cross my palm with silver and I'll tell you.' She spluttered a laugh. Billy laughed too and pulled away his hands. And then he looked at her again, his eyes so steady she saw herself bending forward in the black of them to hear what he had to say.

'I'll build this fair up again, as good as me da ran it. Better. Bring the punters back and start making real money for everyone again. That's what'll happen.'

'It will if you believe it, my love,' she said and stroked his hair.

'Aye. And Webster'll be the start of it. People'll come from miles to see him and what he is.'

'Yes, they will.'

'Even Da. He'll be so shocked, what's left of him'll crawl out of that grave we laid him in two years ago to see for himself. And then I'll tell him he was wrong to say I couldn't run the fair as good as him. He'll eat his words. The same way that cancer ate through his bones and left him limp as an empty grain sack.'

Outside, the machinery had stopped. The fair had been dismantled and packed away, ready for the next town. The silence was perfect. And within it Billy imagined a future of his very own making that was perfect too.

17

James read the newspaper headline in the bottom corner of the page with great interest.

Missing Boy

His picture was below it. In colour. The gold on the lapels of his school blazer gleaming. The photograph had been taken before the world had changed forever. James remembered his mother wetting her thumb and wiping away a smudge from his cheek before the camera clicked and the photographer said, 'Perfect!' The smile had dropped clean off his face after that, defaulting back to a frown. On the bus journey home she had told him to grow up because everyone had to do things they didn't like doing occasionally. That was life. And James had sat on the plastic seat, fuming, not saying anything at all. Wishing the world to hell.

The man holding the newspaper folded it round to the next page, making it crackle, and James looked away.

He paid for the cups of tea and carried them over to Webster who was sitting in the window, watching the street. James's hands shook as he walked and tea spilt over into the white saucers. But no one noticed him as he walked through snippets of conversation and the scraping of cutlery on plates.

'I'm in the paper,' he said quietly as he sat down.

'Fame at last,' said Webster and smiled.

They said nothing else as they sipped their tea. No one bothered them. But James looked away every time he caught someone's eye.

'Got any way of explaining it?' asked Webster.

'What?'

Webster raised his hands.

'It. The world.'

'No.'

Webster pursed his lips.

'Well, let me know if you do.'

Other customers ate. Drank. Talked. Came and went. Eventually, Webster started muttering under his breath, drumming his hands on the table. The odd person began to look up, making James nervous.

'There isn't just one world,' he said quietly. 'There's billions.'

Webster stopped his muttering and edged forward in his seat.

'How do you mean?'

'Everyone's standing on their own world, spinning round each other, trying not to collide.'

James could not think of anything more to add. Webster just nodded and said nothing. He went back to staring calmly into space and nobody bothered to look at him any more.

When James noticed a newspaper lying on an empty table, he walked over to it and picked it up, and sat back down. His life was summed up in two small paragraphs which did not take long to read. He knew everything already. That he lived in Timpston, which was hidden deep in a green fold of Devon. That his mother had died in a car crash. That he lived with his stepfather.

But there was a lot about his life that wasn't there at all. After reading it through a couple of times, he tore out his picture. Folded it up. And put it in his pocket along with his notes.

He scanned the rest of the page. And then he held it up for Webster.

'See?' he said. 'Billions.'

Webster looked at the page, and then at the boy, and nodded.

*   *   *

103

It was dusk by the time they left the café to look for a motel. When Webster caught sight of the moon rising at the far end of the street, he stopped. It was big and bright. A row of two-up two-downs hummed on either side of them.

'Here,' said James, 'I found this.' And he took out a square of newspaper which he unfolded and gave to Webster. 'We've got less time than we thought.'

Webster stared at the details on the piece of paper, and saw the listing of the times of sunrise and sunset, and the date of the next full moon. He kept staring as though expecting the date to change. But it didn't.

'Three days isn't long, is it?' he said eventually.

'It's long enough,' said James.

Webster looked up at the moon again. He breathed as slowly as he was able.

'What makes a man, do you think?'

'I don't know,' said James. Webster rubbed his brow. Planted his hands on the crown of his head.

'Things would be a whole lot simpler if we did.'

When they started walking again, Webster noticed a figure standing in a deep, dark doorway on the opposite side of the street, smoking a cigarette. The shadows were too strong to see the face clearly. Smoke was gathered like wool around it. He thought nothing of it at first because he was too busy thinking about the future. But, when he looked back after a few paces, the person was gone.

His blood sharpened. He looked out of the corners of his eyes to see more clearly in the moonlight.

'We're going to split up at the end of the street,' he said quietly. When James stopped to ask him why, he laid an arm around the boy's shoulders and pushed him on. 'Keep walking,' he whispered. James did as he was told, eyes flicking from side to side. He was unsure exactly who, or even what, he was looking for. And then he realized. Something dark licked up into the back of his throat and he swallowed it down.

'It's them, isn't it? How did they find us?'

'I don't know, but it's me they want,' said Webster as they neared the end of the street. 'Go. I'll meet you back at the car. Wait out of sight until I get there.' James nodded without looking up as they parted on the corner.

Eventually, he glanced back.

Webster was gone.

James kept going, planning a route back to the car in his head. When he reached the end of the street, he waited for a bus to pass. The engine noise caught between the gaps in his bones and made him shudder.

'Hello, boy,' said a voice. A warm hand gripped the back of James's neck before he could turn around. Hot breath cooled in the whorl of his ear. 'I told ya. I never forget a face.' The hand left James's neck. Something sharp pushed up into his spine. 'I'll pull the trigger if you so much as make a squeak.'

When he heard a growl beside him, James looked down. A big black dog was staring up at him, teeth bared, straining on a metal chain.

18

Webster walked quickly through the moonlight without looking back. Eventually, rounding a third corner, he stopped and lay flat against the wall of a house. Street lamps dropped down cones of orange light that shimmered as he breathed.

Moments later, a man appeared. Walking fast.

Webster caught him square in the face with a fist and heard the nose crack. His knuckles were still ringing as the man dropped to the ground and a shotgun clattered to the pavement from beneath his long waxed coat.

Webster picked up the gun. Listened for a moment.

Nothing except for the man cursing into his hands. Something black was trickling between his fingers as he rolled from side to side. Webster brought down the butt of the shotgun on the back of his head. Then, in the silence that followed, he listened again.

The sound of a television burbling.

A cat mewling outside a door.

The beating of his heart.

He opened the neck of the shotgun. Two red cartridges with their copper-coloured ends. He clicked the gun shut and listened again, then rolled the man over with his boot.

It wasn't Billy.

It was Swanney.

His eyes fluttered open and he looked up at Webster from either side of his broken nose, and swore and spat and kicked out. Webster's finger tightened on the trigger. A great screw seemed to turn in his jaw, hardening it. There were clean, gleaming thoughts about what he should do next. They seemed without question, or consequence, as the trigger grew big against his finger.

But then his arm began to shake.

The harsh metal smell of the gun came up at him in waves. Suddenly, the trigger was so hot he had to let go. His brow was burning. Wet. He tried to wipe it clean.

'I knew you was touched,' growled Swanney. Webster was shaking. Blinking faster as his eyes began to sting with sweat. Swanney's legs and arms seemed to be lengthening. Unwinding. Reaching out for him. 'I knew it!'

Webster took a step back. He guessed that Swanney was standing up, but he was blinking too quickly to see.

And then he felt hands grabbing the opposite end of the shotgun.

Webster ripped the gun free. Tottered backwards. And the shock of it cleared his head.

Swanney was standing there in front of him, his bloody smile falling away as Webster levelled the gun at his chest.

A window opened along the street. Somebody shouted and cut the silence in half and, when Webster half looked, it set Swanney loose. He turned and ran, disappearing round the corner.

There was a squeal of brakes.

A dull thump.

The sound of an engine idling.

Webster edged around the corner. Swanney was lying face down on the pavement, his waist perfectly in line with the kerb, a dark puddle forming quickly around his head, or what was left of it, the back of its sphere missing, like a rotten windfall apple scooped out to its core. The headlights of the car shone straight down the road.

The engine wobbled and died.

The driver's door opened.

And somebody leant out and retched.

Webster retreated back around the corner and walked on quickly, the gun hidden beneath his great-coat. His skin was hot, his lungs full of sparks. And gradually the night air slipped inside his chest and cooled him.

As he wound a path back to the car, he stopped every now and then. But there was nobody following him. He was sure of it. Because there was nobody reflected in the shop windows or the wing mirrors of cars as he passed them by. Yet he knew Billy had to be somewhere. Billy, who had found him, and locked him in the wagon cage like an animal.

And then Webster began to worry about the boy.

When he was close, he stopped in the adjoining street and listened carefully, but all he heard was the silence. He rounded the corner, the shotgun tight against his hip beneath the greatcoat.

Street lamps dipped their necks like swans.

He saw houses, in a row, on either side. Set back from the street. With paths dissecting tiny gardens, which lead up to each front door.

James was not waiting by the car.

Webster walked on, straight past it, when he saw the slashed tyres slumped against the kerb like snowmelt. James's duffel bag of clothes was sitting on the front seat, his black suit draped on top. But Webster did not waver. He was light inside. Like a ghost. Or something made of paper. Somewhere in the dark a dog was barking and the sound of it chimed in the marrow of his bones.

The crunch of his boots on the pavement became hypnotic. For a moment, it took him somewhere else. Back into the past. Into a desert shimmer. He heard shouting. Mortar fire. Gunshots. The barking of dogs. He felt the sun and the dust on his face from a foreign land. He could smell sweat and boot polish and webbing and sun-kissed rock. The gun filled out forgotten parts of his hand as he gripped it tighter and tighter.

He stopped, his breathing hard in his ears.

A growl was rolling towards him.

A large black dog tore out of the dark. Tongue trailing. Claws hissing on the pavement.

But Webster was not scared. He brought up the shotgun and fired once into the chest of the creature as it leapt for him.

It yelped. Landed across the tops of his boots. The warm weight of it lodged against his shins.

A bedroom light came on across the road, followed by others. Curtains twitched. Webster stepped over the dog and kept moving. The end of the street swallowed him up as people came out of their houses and crowded round the dead black dog, stepping back from the blood as it pooled out over the pavement.

19

When Billy saw Webster raise the shotgun and shoot the dog dead, he knew that Swanney was not going to appear and help him.

As Webster kept walking towards the end of the street, Billy dragged James away, slipping down an alley where large steel bins were piled high with black plastic bags. At the far end, he followed the cobbles round to the left and found himself on a narrow path that wound round between high-walled buildings and then opened up into a square ringed with cars. On three sides were tall, smart houses, set back from the road, with large bay windows and black railings like lines of spears. On the one open side was the fringe of a green park lit by street lights.

Somewhere in the distance a police siren skewered the air. As it faded, a gunshot ripped through the car nearest to Billy and James, blowing out a window. Billy's blood shuddered in the wind of it. Something sharp caught the side of his face, and he put up a hand and felt a shard of glass lodged in his cheek like a tooth in the wrong place. His stomach turned and he looked back.

Webster had dropped the shotgun and was running towards them. Billy drew James closer to him, putting the pistol to the boy's head.

'Stop!' shouted Billy. But Webster kept on coming. Mouth open. Roaring. Tongue straining at its root. Billy raised the pistol and fired into the sky. But Webster did not falter.

Billy felt James shaking. He was shaking too. Flinging the boy to the ground, he turned and ran into the park, disappearing into the dark.

James was a heap in the road. His head had gone off like another gunshot on striking the tarmac. Glass tumbled from his hair as Webster picked him up in his arms and carried him away from the square. He did not stop, keeping to the small paths and alleyways. Eventually, he found a towpath and followed the canal until he came to a bridge. He laid the boy down underneath the arch and then took off his greatcoat and wrapped him in it.

James's face was cut in places. Blood had dried in sticky patches. Webster ripped a corner from his shirt and used the water from the old plastic bottle in his greatcoat pocket to wipe the boy's face clean. After emptying the bottle, he stopped and stared at it, and squashed the sides together, and yelled and hurled it away down the path. Then he took out the small glass jar of ointment from another pocket and ran his little finger round the inside until he had enough paste to smear across the cuts on James's face.

After he had finished, Webster listened for some time to the distant buzz of a helicopter, and watched the spotlight strobe back and forth over the rooftops of the town.

Eventually, he lost interest and stared at the moon. He cursed at it under his breath until the anger in him had died down, leaving him cold and hollow inside.

After walking back down the path, he picked up the empty bottle and observed it for some time, turning it through his fingers, before screwing the top back on.

James stirred when Webster knelt beside him and put the bottle back in one of the pockets of the greatcoat. 'Where are we?' he said.

'No place for a boy like you, that's for sure,' said Webster, staring at the black canal water. It could have been a river of blood for all he knew without some sort of light to shine on it and see for sure.

June 12th

20

The bus tucked back its doors like a pair of wings.

Webster stepped down on to the pavement and blinked in the sunlight. James appeared by his side. Just the two of them. A man in a dirty blue greatcoat and a boy in a black waterproof filched from the back of a chair. They stood facing the warped reflection of themselves in the dark glass window of an office.

'So,' said Webster, 'here we are.'

The bus shuddered and growled as it left. Cars zipped by.

'If we go to the exact spot,' said James, 'you might remember something.'

Webster caught sight of a plane in the deep blue between two tall buildings. He watched it until it was gone and there was nothing left but a white trail fattening. He closed his eyes.

'I wish we were somewhere else,' he said.

* * *

They walked until the office blocks on either side of them faded away into a vast park and then they started over a large expanse of grass, which was hard and browned from the sun. Bodies were marooned on towels and rugs. Lifeless-looking. As if their souls had abandoned them. In the mighty distance someone was steering a kite on the breeze.

They kept going for some time without saying anything, Webster plotting the way with James beside him. Eventually, they stopped in the shade of a line of lime trees by the top of a sheer bank that fell away sharply into a long, steep slope. Old magazines, caught in a matting of weeds about halfway down, flapped like dying winged things. A Coke can had burrowed in deep. Great thickets of brambles and hawthorn were fused together at the bottom.

'It was here,' said Webster. 'I fell down this part of the bank.' He pointed and opened his hand as though introducing James to an old friend. They stood in silence, listening to the magazines catching the breeze. Looking into the brambles below.

'Anything?' asked James eventually. Webster stared for a while longer and then shook his head.

James studied the drop beneath them one last time and then looked along the edge of the bank in both directions.

Nothing but trees.

And grass.

And the path trailing off into the distance.

'Doesn't seem like much of a place to meet evil,' he said.

Webster looked around them. And then he bent down and whispered in James's ear.

'The stuff gets everywhere,' he said and then stiffened and straightened, folding his arms, as a crow landed on the grass and bounced towards them. Not a sound as it stopped and stared up at them, head cocked, one black eye shining a half-moon in the sun. Webster raised his arms to shoo it away, but the crow seemed glued to the grass. So he ran at it, shouting and hissing, and James watched it flap its wings and wheel into the sky. It was nothing more than a black dot by the time Webster had started walking away, leaving James to wonder why the man had done such a thing.

After half an hour, they came upon a small kiosk selling cold drinks and ice cream. A fountain hissed in the middle of an ornamental pond and people were perched around the stone rim, cooling off in the damp air.

Webster bought James an ice cream and a cup of tea in a styrofoam cup for himself, and they lay on the hard, baked ground, staring up at the sky, wondering what to do next.

'You don't remember anything at all?' James asked finally.

'No.' Webster let out a long, slow breath. 'Not from that night anyway.' James noticed that Webster's hands were trembling. His tea broke in tiny brown waves inside the cup, which was sitting on top of his chest, rising and falling as he breathed.

'You mean you keep remembering when you were a soldier?'

Webster stared at his hands until they were steady and then he took a sip of his tea.

'Yeah.' He tapped the side of his head. 'Sometimes things pop up out of the dark when I don't expect it. Or if I think too much.'

James nodded because he understood exactly what Webster meant.

'Do you want to talk about that instead?' he asked. Webster said nothing. 'We don't have to if you don't want to.'

'I can't say it really helps,' said Webster.

'We could pretend we're asleep.'

Webster just smiled.

'Not now.'

'OK.'

And James stripped down to his tatty white T-shirt

and balled up his waterproof and sweater behind his head, and lay down and closed his eyes.

When they walked on, they discovered an old man sitting on a bench, scattering nuggets of bread into a cloud of pigeons. James kept staring as they walked towards him because the old man was only using his left hand to dig into the bag of bread and tear each white slice apart, while his right arm lay still on his lap. It made feeding the birds a laborious task. But he stuck to it.

'Lovely afternoon,' said the man with a slight slur to his voice, and James noticed that the right-hand side of his face was drooping more than it should.

Webster just nodded and walked on, but James went over and sat down. There was something about the old man he recognized in himself, sitting there, all alone, as the world passed him by.

'Sore feet,' he said, pointing at his black school shoes as the pigeons moved in an oily shoal around them. The old man chuckled.

'Come far then?' he asked, slapping his left hand on his thigh to clean it, frightening the pigeons and making them skip.

'A way.'

'What's your father doing?'

James smiled as he watched Webster inspecting every

tree and peering into every bin. And then he realized the man was still waiting for an answer.

'We're looking for clues.'

'Oh?' The old man picked up his walking stick, which was leaning against the arm of the bench, and flicked away the nuggets of bread nearest to him with the rubber tip, aiming for the pigeons.

'Somebody attacked him and we're trying to find out who.'

'Attacked your father? Here, in this park?'

'One night a few weeks ago.'

The old man tutted and shook his head as the pigeons pecked and cooed and bobbed.

'Do you sit here a lot?' James asked.

'Yes. My wife and I used to come here every day. We'd talk for hours. Now it's just me of course.' The man cleared his throat before he went on. 'I can't say I've seen anything that'll help you.'

'That's OK.'

They sat in silence, watching people as they passed.

No one spoke to them.

Very few people even looked at them.

'I feel like the Invisible Man,' said James eventually and the old man nodded wistfully.

When Webster returned, he sat beside James on the flat, wooden arm of the bench.

'Anything?' James asked.

'Not a button,' said Webster, shaking his head.

'I'm guessing it was a man who attacked you?' asked the old man.

'Of a sort, I suppose.' And Webster glanced at James, wondering what he'd said.

'It'll come back around to them one day.'

Webster licked his lips. Wiped his brow with the back of his hand. 'Is that how life works?' he asked. 'Somebody gets their comeuppance if they deserve it?'

'I don't know for sure, but I'd like to think so,' the old man replied.

'What if something bad happens that isn't their fault?'

'I couldn't say. Why do you ask?'

'No reason.' Webster looked down at his lap and said nothing more.

'No one really knows anything, do they?' said James to fill the silence, and the old man laughed out loud and the pigeons rippled up into a cloud that glimmered with pinks and blues and browns. He drummed the fingers of his left hand over the top of his walking stick then cleared his throat.

'Where are you staying?' he asked. Webster and James glanced at each other for an answer. 'Because I have a house, which I rattle around in, if you'd like to stay. Until you've found what you're looking for.'

'Are you sure?' asked James.

'If it'll do some good then I'm all for it. I'm not sure there's enough in the world just now. Or, if there is, I'm not seeing it.' He held out his left hand, turning it upside down for James to grasp and shake. 'I'm Cook,' he said.

21

Cook's house was large and set halfway down a road of detached houses with semi-circle driveways and porches that lit up at night.

James lay in bed and listened to the night sounds in the walls and the ceiling. The bed sheets smelt musty. An old bloodstain on one of the white pillow-cases had turned brown over time and seemed to follow him wherever he laid his head. But he just accepted it because he was tired, and the mattress in the bed was soft and seemed to hold every atom of him perfectly.

Cook had been very welcoming. Grilling them steaks he had stored in the freezer. Offering them red wine and telling James to try it because life was too short not to. He showed them pictures of his wife as they sat in the living room afterwards, drinking fresh coffee, and asked after their family.

'We're all there is,' James had replied. Cook had nodded and then asked what line of work Webster was in, and James had told him he had been in the army, which had worn him out, and Cook asked nothing more about it after that.

Webster said nothing the whole time.

Eventually, after speaking and growing easier with each other, the boy plucked up courage to ask about Cook's useless right arm, and the droop in his face, and the old man told him he had suffered a stroke the year before. It made life difficult, he said, but not impossible, and yet not always worth living. James smiled and said he understood what Cook meant.

Later, as James slept, he dreamt of his mother bustling round Cook's house, tidying and cleaning until the surfaces in the kitchen shone and the fitted carpets were sucked clean and bright, and the dust on the mantelpiece in the living room was gone.

When he awoke, it was still night. The moon was almost full and shone through the four panes of glass in the window, printing the ghost of a white kite below it on the bedroom floor. It was difficult to fall back to sleep in a strange house. So James lay there, trying to piece together fragments from his dreaming.

He sat up when he heard someone walking along the landing.

When the footsteps stopped, James listened for a while longer and then got out of bed and opened the door. Webster was perched on the window sill near the top of the stairs, wrapped in a white sheet. He was looking up at the moon. James sat quietly beside him and asked if he was all right.

Webster nodded.

'I thought I heard somebody outside the house, but I didn't see anyone and then I found myself sitting here.'

James stared out of the window at the dark garden below, running his fingers over the faint bobble of scars on his face. The ointment had worked as quickly on him as it had on Webster. But he had given up trying to understand how.

'What'll we do if they find us again?' he asked Webster.

The man said nothing, just wrapped the sheet tighter round him and licked his lips. In the silence they heard Cook starting to snore.

'We should tell him,' said James.

'Or we could just leave.'

James shook his head. 'Cook's lonely. We're doing some good.'

'And he's doing some too, isn't he? So we can't leave, can we?'

'No. We can't.'

Webster rubbed his eyes. 'Let's sleep on it. Decide in the morning.'

'I'm glad you said that.'

'Why?'

'Because I didn't want all this to be a dream and wake up and find myself back in Timpston.'

'You don't ever want to go back, do you?'

'No.'

'Because your stepfather's there?'

James nodded. 'If I had to go back, I wouldn't know what to do.'

'To make things better, you mean?'

'Yes.'

'Maybe you can't.'

James thought about that. 'No,' he said, 'I don't think I can. I reckon I'd have more chance of making it up there.' And he pointed through the window at the moon.

Later that night, Cook awoke with a start. He was not surprised. He barely slept well now, not since the clot in his brain had stuck and rewired him into a different, more decrepit version of himself. He lay staring up at the ceiling. Usually, he felt lonely in the middle of the night when the whole world was asleep. But now, for the first time in a long while, he was not alone.

A noise sent his thoughts skittering away into the dark. He heard it again. The sound of somebody crying out.

Cook levered himself out of bed, and padded to his bedroom door and opened it, following the sound until he came to Webster's door. His hand hovered above the handle as he wondered whether to look in or not.

When he heard another door clicking open, he looked up and saw the boy peering out from the dark of his bedroom.

'It's the war,' said James quietly as he tiptoed on to the landing. 'It's all locked up in there.' He tapped the side of his head.

Webster cried out again. Words burbled into one another.

'Will he settle?' asked Cook and James nodded. 'War does terrible things to people. Turns them into somebody different.'

'Like a stroke can?'

'Yes,' said Cook. 'In a way. The same as grief can too.' And when he looked down at the floor James knew not to ask anything more.

Gradually, the cries ceased. James and Cook stood like sentinels guarding the door until the silence began to hum.

'He'll be OK now,' said James. So Cook nodded and returned to his bedroom after whispering goodnight.

* * *

Back in bed, James lay thinking about what Cook had said. About how Webster might have been turned into somebody else because of the war and how different he might have been before then, before they had ever met. And James wondered if he could ever help change him back.

Eventually, he clicked on the bedside light and took out the notes from the back pocket of his jeans, which were hanging over the back of a chair, and read a section over and over. Throughout history there had been some people who had truly believed in the ability of men or women to shape-shift into terrible creatures on the night of a full moon, but there were far more who had proclaimed it to have been a delusion of those diagnosed as mad or sad or troubled.

No one knew the truth for sure.

After James had finished reading, he slipped the notes back into the pocket of his jeans and turned out the light. The dark held him gently in the palm of its hand. Yet he could not sleep. His mind kept turning over what he knew to be real about the world and what was not. And the more he mulled it over, the less sure he became of anything at all. In the end he tried telling himself that whatever he thought did not matter in the slightest.

But, deep down, he knew it did.

June 13th

22

When Cook picked up the newspaper, from beneath the letter box at the base of the front door, he saw James's picture on the front page. Webster was standing back down the hallway, watching him, the morning sunshine beaming off his black hair. The old man laid the paper flat on the dresser by the door and scanned it. When he sensed someone watching him, he looked up.

'The boy's here of his own free will,' said Webster. 'He's got no one else.'

Cook tapped the newspaper.

'Says he's got a stepfather worried sick.'

'He beats him.'

'So you're his saviour?'

'And he's mine. Same as we're yours.'

Cook smiled at that.

James appeared at the top of the stairs and powered down them. He stopped when he saw the newspaper lying on the dresser. Both men were staring at him.

'Someone'll notice you eventually,' said Cook. 'And then there'll be trouble.'

'No one has yet,' James said.

'They will around here. It's that sort of place.'

'Do you want us to leave?' asked James.

'That's up to you.'

Webster and James looked at each other and something passed between them.

'We'll stay,' said Webster. 'For another day. We'll need to leave then anyway, even if we don't find who we're looking for.'

'Why?' asked Cook.

'Because then it'll be out of our hands.'

When Cook looked at James to ask why, the boy just turned away, saying nothing.

They decided James should stay with Cook while Webster went back to the park to look around again for clues. As they drank tea, Cook described how he had been divorced early on in his life, but then found his real love second time around.

'Luck, I used to call it,' he said. 'Fate, she used to say. I don't mind telling you, if there's a plan for each of us, I reckon I got a better one than most. I'm not sure what

I did to deserve it. Maybe *that* was luck.' And he chuckled.

James told Cook stories about school.

They avoided the real questions weighing inside them. And they knew it. But that was how it was.

After a few moments of silence staring into the brown dregs in the bottom of the teacups, Cook slapped his thigh and asked if James would like to see his garden, and the boy nodded. Both of them were glad for the chance to have something else to talk about.

The garden shone. It moved and lived around them as they walked down the green, striped lawn. Cook used his walking stick to point out the various trees and shrubs his wife had planted, at the shapes she had sculpted using flower beds and borders. And James began to imagine what sort of person she might have been.

They followed the sound of running water and stood by a shallow stream flowing down the left-hand side of the garden. Green weed like streamers. Flat stones silvered with bubbles. Cook leant on his stick and grinned at the tiny fish hovering, gulping water over their gills.

James could tell he was proud of the garden and even prouder of his wife.

'It's lovely,' he said and Cook beamed.

'All I can do is to try and keep it ticking over the way she would have wanted.'

'To remember her by?'

135

Cook nodded.

'She used to spend all her time out here. She would say all the clues you ever needed were here.'

'Clues? About what?'

Cook smiled. He beckoned James over to a flower with red petals and a black cushion of a centre. And then he told him to crouch down and look the flower full in the face.

'Can you see what she meant?'

James stared. Squinted. Half nodded. 'Maybe . . .' And then he shook his head. 'No. I'm not sure what you mean.'

'You will. When you're ready. Just like I did.'

James tried again, focusing on the flower's black centre, which had the texture of velvet. The hum of insects began to fade. And somehow, as though a spell had been cast over him, he was filled with a sense of hope. The idea of it seemed so fragile he could not describe it to Cook, fearful it might break apart with the weight of words.

When the moment left him, leaving just a notion like a vapour in his head, James looked up to ask more about it.

'You should go inside,' said Cook, nodding up at something over the boy's shoulder. 'They're all nosy parkers around here.'

When James looked round, he saw the face of a middle-aged woman disappearing from a bedroom window in the house next door. Before he could ask about the neighbour, a bird flapped across his eyeline, landing on the branch of a nearby tree. The crow looked down, studying them like a person might, and it seemed to darken a spot in James's heart although he wasn't sure why. He raised his arms and hissed, and the bird took off, flying low over the fence and disappearing. Breathing hard, all James could think was that Webster would have done exactly the same.

Cook was looking at him.

'They're bad luck,' said James before the old man could ask him anything.

After the boy had gone back inside, Cook pottered in the garden without his walking stick, deadheading flowers as well as he was able, throwing the old brown heads into a basket hanging from a cord slung diagonally across his chest. When he reached the far end of the garden, he stopped and mopped his brow with a white handkerchief that bore the blue stitching of his initials in one corner. Retreating into the shade of a willow, he stood admiring everything around him. He was comforted by the presence of every tree for he knew that, in his old age, he would never have to say goodbye to them as he had done to his wife and so many of their friends.

It took ten minutes until he was cool again and the hammer of his heart in his head had vanished.

As he turned to walk back to the house, he heard a sobbing, from beyond the cedar fence at the end of the garden, which backed on to the lane. Cook slid back the bolt on the door and stepped out on to the shimmering black asphalt. Insects buzzed in the heat in flimsy clouds. The verges on either side of the lane were stacked with tall grasses and coloured with wild flowers, as though a rainbow had cracked and fallen to the earth in shards. A woman of roughly his own age was standing at the side of the road, bent over, staring at something in the grass that Cook could not see. As she dabbed her eyes with a handkerchief, the leather pouch dangling from its cord around her neck swung gently from side to side.

'Are you all right, my dear?' he asked her.

When she saw him, with his droopy mouth and his basket of deadheads hanging from his chest, she pointed at the verge beside her, saying nothing.

In between the weave of stems and roots, Cook saw a dead blackbird. Like a drop of tar, its beak two yellow triangles set slightly apart.

As he stared, he began to lose the sense of the heat of the world around him until all he knew was a profound sadness licking his insides cold. It was as though he had caught his unhappiness from the woman beside him. He shivered as he looked into the bird's black eye and could not help but think about the corpse of his wife when he had found her in the garden that day.

'I don't know what came over me,' said the woman, wiping her face with her sleeve. 'But it's just so . . . well, it's just so sad.'

Cook nodded.

'It is.' He tried to say more, but he had no breath. He wiped a cold, thick sweat from his brow. The woman smiled and touched his arm. The dark inside him broke apart and he felt the heat of the sun on his neck again, the beats of it coming up off the road into his face. He smiled back at her.

'Can I offer you a cup of tea?' he said and blushed.

She toyed with the little leather pouch around her neck and Cook thought he heard something tinkling inside.

'Only if I can make it for you, dear,' she replied, picking up her red leather bag, sitting half hidden in the grass, and hitching it over her shoulder. Cook nodded without even thinking. The darkness in him had been replaced by a sense of joy. And then he realized why.

It would be just like having his wife in the house again.

23

'I'm Esther,' she said to James as he stared at her grey gums and rickety teeth. Webster had warned him to be on the lookout for anything odd or strange. But it was Cook who had invited her into his house, assuring the boy it was fine and telling him how sad the woman had been in the lane.

'Where are you from?' he asked as she bustled about the kitchen, the kettle close to boiling, the brown leather pouch around her neck clinking against her chest. She found the mugs without asking where they were and James wondered if it had been luck or not.

'Oh, down the lane. What about you, dear?'

'I'm visiting my grandfather,' he said, but the old woman kept staring, waiting for the answer to her question. 'I'm from a village in the middle of nowhere,' said James and shrugged. She nodded then pointed at Cook sitting out on the patio, admiring the garden.

'You can tell your grandfather the tea's nearly ready.'

After James had left the kitchen, she undid the zip on the small outside pocket of her red leather bag and took out a bouquet of herbs and grasses which she pushed into the white teapot. Then she poured in the hot water from the kettle and secured the lid.

As she did so, something moved inside the main body of her bag, squirming and making the sides bulge, but she gently shushed whatever was in there and the red leather stopped creaking.

They all sat on the patio in the sun.

James and Cook drank a mug of tea each, and they tasted vanilla and mint and sunshine, and both of them approved. They listened to the old woman's stories about herself as a girl and how different the world had been when she was young. At one point, James found he was not really listening any more. He looked over at Cook and saw him laughing, agreeing with everything being said. And then, quite suddenly, a drop of blood appeared, wobbling at the edge of one of the old man's nostrils. Before James could say anything, the woman leant forward and wiped it away with a paper napkin without missing a beat of what she was saying. James wondered about what he had seen. Questions inside him immediately gave rise to others.

He turned to ask the woman who she really was.

But the words burst in his throat as he opened his mouth. He gagged on them and, as he caught his breath, all he could manage was to look up at her.

She was muttering to herself, one hand clutching her leather pouch, the fingers rippling back and forth. He tried to hear what she was saying, but his ears were full of the drone of insects and the ticking of the sun on the patio table and chairs.

Cook had stopped laughing. His left hand was clamped to his head as he rocked gently back and forth in his chair.

James leant forward across the table and stared into the old woman's eyes. When she smiled, James knew that all the good around him had been sucked clean away. He heard someone laughing and followed the sound until he saw the painted face of a small wooden man, peering up out of the red leather bag, its hands gripping the top.

James tried to cry out.

But he could not make a sound.

She took James and Cook by the hand, and led them into the house and sat them on the sofa in the living room. Then she bound their wrists with lengths of washing line which she had unhooked from the two wooden posts in the garden. When she was satisfied that all was in order, she drew out a mobile phone and tapped out a text message with one bony finger. And then she knelt down in front of James.

'What are you doing here, my darling?'

James struggled to speak. It was difficult to focus on her. He wanted to tell the old woman the exact truth, but all he could manage was spit and hot air. She muttered something under her breath and then laid a hand on his knee. A weight released inside him. The fog in his head cleared. He was able to speak.

'We're looking for whoever attacked Webster,' he said.

'And why's you doing that, my love?'

'So Webster can forgive whoever's done him wrong and cure himself of evil. Forgiving is the only way to do it. That's what the vicar in the church said.' The old woman smiled.

'Hmmm,' she purred. 'I'm not sure it'll make any difference, my darling.'

When she took her hand away from his knee, James felt his throat closing, as if someone was pulling a thread tight around it.

After she had clicked the door shut behind her, he tried screaming out loud for someone to hear. But it was impossible to make a sound.

When his mother appeared on the floor in front of him, bloody and broken like a corpse, he tried to speak to her and ask for help. But all James could manage were tiny grunts like the noise of some shuffling thing at night in the leaf litter of a forest.

She crawled up on to the seat beside him and held the boy until he closed his eyes and lost himself in her arms. She began whispering that he should never have left home, constantly so, until James tried to wish her away, saying that she wasn't real. But she told him she was and that he did not really want her to leave at all. And, in the end, he just nodded and said nothing else as she kept berating him in her soft, gentle voice until the dark of her embrace swallowed him up.

24

'Jesus, Ma, whatchoo done to them?'

'Don't you fret at yer mother,' she said, slapping Billy on the meat of his arm. 'They're fine as we want them for now.'

Billy crouched down in front of the sleeping Cook. The lines on his face were so deep it seemed he might break apart at any moment.

'He's old. Look at him.'

'Stop fussing.'

Billy reached forward and touched Cook on the wrists as though venerating him.

'I won't ever get like this,' he said, lifting the old man's hands and inspecting them before laying them carefully back down on his knees.

His mother clapped three times and muttered something, and touched Cook on the elbow. His eyes flickered open. He licked his lips. Blinked. Shuddered.

145

'Tell him what's going to happen,' she said to Billy as she shuffled out.

It took a few moments for Cook to come round fully and for his cheeks to fill with colour. When he understood what was happening to himself and the boy, who was still asleep beside him, he began to struggle, the waxy knots of the washing line squeaking as they rubbed. Billy watched him, sitting cross-legged on the floor. He took a penknife from his pocket and pulled out the blade from the brown wooden handle and began cleaning his fingernails, flicking black dirt on to the carpet.

'What do you want?' asked Cook eventually.

'How long have you got?' replied Billy and grinned.

'I don't have any money in the house.'

'I know,' said Billy, shrugging.

'Who are you?'

'A man, like you, but beyond that then we're both struggling, en't we?'

'Let my grandson go.'

'He en't yer grandson.'

Cook watched Billy move on to the other set of nails.

'What do you want with them?'

'It's Webster we want. The boy's just bait.' Billy raised his eyebrows as something occurred to him. 'For now anyway.'

'What's Webster done?'

'It's what's been done to him is more important.'

'What do you mean by that?'

But Billy did not seem to hear the question.

'Yoo'se gonna speak to him when he comes back. Tell him he's coming with us because he's got no choice. Because we got the boy.' Billy winced as the tip of the knife went in too deep beneath a nail. 'And we don't want him hurting himself neither or doing nothing stupid. Webster's a valuable man to us. Special.'

Billy reached for a holdall on the floor beside the sofa and drew out a pair of handcuffs which he laid on the glass coffee table in front of Cook.

'He's to lock himself up in these.'

'What if he doesn't want to?'

Billy shrugged.

'My ma is the one who'll do it. She's got those skills. And she won't have an ounce of guilt if it comes to using them on the boy.'

Cook thought about that. He tried to swallow, but his mouth was dry.

'Webster's his own man. He won't do what I say.'

'Then you'll both be to blame for what happens to the boy.' Billy placed the penknife down on the coffee table away from the handcuffs. 'The world's a tough old place for sure,' he sighed, 'but I reckon you know that better than me.' He set the penknife spinning on the glass top and watched the blade flashing back the daylight. 'I know you en't always lived here on yer own. Not in this big old house.' Billy grinned and lowered his voice. 'My ma can still smell her in the curtains and the furniture.' The knife stopped, the blade pointing directly at Cook. 'We all take our turn eventually, don't we? En't nothing we can do about that.'

Cook stared at the penknife. And then looked away, remembering his wife. Her golden hair. The shape of her mouth. The pinch of the Cupid's bow. The hollow in the small of her back where he would lay his hand.

'You tell Webster to stay nice and calm. We want him without a scratch. He's a special man.'

'So you keep saying,' said Cook. 'What's so special about him?'

Billy smiled. Folded his arms.

'He was attacked on the night of a full moon.'

'So?'

When Billy saw Cook's blank stare, he threw back his head and howled at the ceiling, his throat gobbling like a turkey's. Cook began shaking his head as soon as he realized.

'He's got the marks to prove it,' said Billy, 'the story to tell too. That's why he's come back here. To try and undo what happened to him in the park before we found him and made him ours. My ma's seen it and the boy told her too when she asked him. Webster's got this notion he can forgive the creature what attacked him so he don't become one neither.' Billy smiled. 'They spoke to a priest about it.' He shrugged as though it was all beyond him. 'I en't so sure there's any way to undo what's happened.' He picked up the penknife and folded the blade away, stowing it in his trouser pocket. And then he looked up at Cook and smiled. 'Just like there en't no way of bringing yer wife back to the world neither.'

After Billy had left, Cook sat for a long time, pondering what he believed to be true about the world and what he did not. About Webster. And about the old woman too.

Eventually, James awoke and Cook described everything Billy had told him. When he finished, the boy bowed his head.

'I'm sorry. We didn't mean for this to happen. We should never have stayed with you.'

'Do you really believe that Webster was attacked by something most people think belongs in stories?'

'Don't you?'

Cook sighed and shook his head. James looked away and said nothing.

'What does he remember about that night in the park?' asked Cook.

'Not much.'

'I think he only believes he was attacked by something terrifying because that's what these people want him to believe.'

James tried moving his wrists because they were sore. The washing line creaked. His mind ticked over.

And over.

'No,' he said eventually, shaking his head. 'He must have been attacked. There are two scars on his back. Claw marks. I've seen them.'

Cook looked round the room and nodded over at the small round table beside the window. 'See that newspaper? The local one?'

James nodded.

'Have a look at the whole of the front page,' Cook said to him.

James rocked back and forth and lurched up off the sofa. He worked his way over to the table, and bent down over the newspaper. A headline ran across the lower section of the page:

Third Knife Attack In Local Park This Month

He read the whole article, and then he shuffled back to Cook and sat down on the sofa.

'Last night,' he said eventually, 'what you said about war. Can it change people enough to make them believe in things that aren't true?'

'I think it probably can, yes.'

'Can they ever change back?'

But Cook didn't know what to say.

James touched his face and felt the tiny bumps of the scars on his cheeks, and remembered how Webster had used the ointment to heal him.

'I've seen things that don't make sense,' he said, 'but they were definitely real. What about the old woman? The things she's done to us?'

Cook shook his head.

'I don't know how to explain what she's done or the things you say you've seen,' he said.

James tried not to think about anything because it was too confusing to know what to believe or what he wished to be true for Webster. So he ran his eyes round the living room, over the furniture and the walls and the windows, happy just to see things for what they were.

Then something occurred to him.

'It doesn't matter what *we* believe, does it?' he said.

Cook thought about that. And then he nodded. 'You mean as long as Webster finds the person he thinks attacked him then he can cure himself by forgiving them, and hang whatever we think.'

'Yes,' said James. 'As long as he forgives them like the vicar told us. Then the travellers wouldn't want him any more. Not if Webster tells them he's cured. They'd leave us all alone.' James sighed and closed his eyes,

151

trying not to think too hard about what he might be saying about Webster.

Cook could see the tiny pulse in the boy's throat. All he could think about was how, when he had been young, the rest of the world had always taken care of itself. But now, it seemed to him, children were plugged directly into everything in it, the evil as well as the good. He remembered what Webster had said about James, that his stepfather beat him. That James and Webster were friends because the boy had no one else.

He cleared his throat. 'Webster's looking for me,' he said quietly. James sat up and stared at him. Cook could see himself in the black marble stones of the boy's eyes. 'I'm the one Webster needs to forgive. You have to tell him.'

'It doesn't matter if I believe you or not, does it?' James whispered.

'No.'

And James took a deep breath and nodded.

'OK then.' And he looked down at his knees, saying nothing for a while, thinking about Webster and the war. 'We need to escape,' he said eventually. 'Find Webster. So we can tell him.'

'The windows,' said Cook. 'Maybe we can get out that way.'

But, before James could even stand up, the door opened. Billy stood there, looking at them.

'Thought I heard voices,' he said.

He made sure their wrists were still bound tight. Then he ran his hands over the two big windows to check they were secure. When he turned back to the old man and the boy sitting on the sofa, he stared at them for a while.

Eventually, he pulled them to their feet and walked them towards the door.

'Let's have a change of scenery,' he said. 'Yoo'se must be bored stiff sitting here.'

25

It made no difference whether Cook's eyes were open or shut. The blackness was just the same. Deep and impenetrable. Unwinding him into nothing. He kept on reminding himself what he was.

A man.

A man in a cellar.

A man in a cellar in the dark.

But uncomfortable thoughts still flickered up inside him. He had to keep telling himself that death would never be like this. And he did this until he was no longer afraid.

'We need to get out,' said James from somewhere out of the void.

'We will,' said Cook. 'Just stay where you are.'

He started to shuffle, slowly, with his hands bound, because the dark threatened to trip him up and send him spinning. His mind kept up its tricks. It told him, if he lost his footing now, he might never stop falling.

It took Cook ten minutes to work out which wall he had bumped into. He slid slowly to his left and found nothing so then he moved to the right. Just cold brickwork at first and then something hard struck him in the ribs, just below his right armpit. Unsure at first what it might be, he moved his right leg gingerly until his shin hit something else. His thigh bumped something too, almost simultaneously. Cook guessed that he must have found one end of the wooden shelves he had attached to the wall when he had first moved into the house. Now they served a different purpose, as his guide. He slid down their wooden edges and came to their sharp corners. Then he worked his way carefully over the front of the shelves. Something wobbled. A jam jar maybe. He smelt turpentine. Oil. Rust.

After negotiating the shelves, he kept going round the wall to the right, mapping his position in his head.

When something soft touched his face and clung to him, he panicked and stepped back from the wall. It was a moment before he realized it must be a cobweb, the dead, hard bodies of tiny creatures draped over his lips. He sucked it all in then spat and waited in the pitch dark for his blood to cool.

Unsure which way he was facing, he asked James to call out.

The wall was behind him.

Cook turned around and shuffled back to it, connecting up the ends of his toes. He lay against the musty brickwork for a quite a while, listening to the boy whispering softly to him in the dark. When James asked if he was all right, Cook said yes and started moving again.

He came to a corner, shuffled round the right angle and then pressed his body as flat as possible to the wall. He knew it was not much further. When his chest bumped up against the light switch, he lowered himself down until his chin slid on to the button. He pressed it down.

The strip light blinked and flickered on.

They said nothing at first.

It was enough to see each other.

They searched the cellar for anything to cut the washing line around their wrists. But it was difficult without the full use of their hands.

They used their elbows.

Their faces.

Their mouths and feet.

Working clumsily but quietly.

Looking through cardboard boxes.

In tea chests. Under blankets. On shelves.

There were magazines in stacks.

Jars of pennies. Old clothes in bin bags. Nails in tins. Paint pots with their lids glued down hard.

James asked Cook to check his watch. It was three-thirty.

'Webster will be back soon,' said the boy. Cook nodded. They had found nothing to help them.

James began to rub the washing line around his wrists backwards and forwards over a nail protruding from the wall. Cook watched him until he gave up and slumped against the brickwork.

'I might know a way to get us out of here,' said Cook.

When they had agreed on what to do, James walked across the cellar and managed to pick up the small can of oil from the basket on the front of a bicycle that Cook's wife had used a long time ago. He tilted it slowly.

'How much in there?' asked Cook.

'About half.' He held it out to the old man. 'Can you help me with the cap?' It was stuck tight, but they managed to prise it off. And then James tiptoed up the stairs.

He put his ear against the cellar door and listened to the rest of the house. Just a gentle creaking in the walls. He did not bother twisting the handle. Billy had locked the door after turning off the light.

James took a step back down and then aimed the nozzle of the can at the topmost stair and squeezed a golden arc on to the old wood. The oil pooled like treacle and then began to spread, making the grain shine. A sticky finger dripped down on to the stair below.

There was enough for the first five steps. James soaked as much of the wood as he was able.

When the can was empty, he walked quietly back down the stairs and pushed a tea chest across the floor with his knees until it was underneath the strip light. Then he picked up a screwdriver from a shelf and wobbled up on to the top of the chest.

'Wait,' said Cook. After struggling to pick up a small black torch with a rubber grip, he managed to click in the orange button with his thumb and the bulb shone. Then he turned it off and moved to the bottom of the stairs.

'OK. Watch out for the glass. And the powder.'

James nodded and steadied himself before jabbing the end of the screwdriver into the strip light.

Nothing but black again and the after-image of the cellar fading slowly in front of their eyes.

Cook soon lost his sense of where everything was after the boy had crouched down on the tea chest and slipped back on to the floor.

'Are you OK?' he whispered.

'Fine. You?'

'Yes.'

Neither of them said anything else as they waited, trying not to think about what the dark meant to each of them in their own peculiar way.

26

When he heard the key clicking round in the door, Cook felt his blood thicken.

'This is it,' he whispered. He heard James's breathing, the shuffling of his feet, and Cook guessed he was standing up.

The door at the top of the stairs opened. Framed in the pale light of the doorway stood Billy. All James and Cook heard was the sound of the light switch snicking up and down. And then it stopped.

'Webster's on his way, me ma says,' announced Billy from the top of the stairs. 'We need you up here, old man.' Cook bit his lip. Said nothing. Didn't move.

But Billy didn't move either.

Cook kept waiting. 'I need some help up,' he said.

But still Billy did not come down the stairs.

Suddenly James cried out.

'You can't do this!' he shouted. 'Webster! Webster! We're down here!'

'He can't hear you,' said Billy from the top of the stairs. 'He's still a way off, so shut up.'

'Webster!' screamed James so loudly that the deep black corners of the cellar seemed to vibrate.

'Shut up,' hissed Billy.

And then he took a step down.

Immediately, his foot slipped and shot out in front of him as if someone was yanking it up on a string. The dark line of his standing leg crooked, then wilted, and an arm whipped out towards the wall for balance. Four splayed fingers and a thumb.

There was a click. The torch beamed a white tunnel up the staircase with Billy gasping at the end of it. His face crumpled. Both palms came up. And then he skidded forward as though a giant hand had pushed him without warning.

He thumped down the stairs and landed in a silent heap at the bottom.

Cook held the torch as steady as he could, watching the body steaming dust motes into the light. And then his mind was whirring.

'He has a knife.'

James dropped to his knees and started fumbling through Billy's pockets, not stopping his frantic search until he had found the penknife.

'Hold out your hands,' he said to Cook.

Cook did so, as well as he was able. And James took the torch and stood it between his feet to give him enough light. At first, the blade slipped on the waxy skin of the washing line because it was not jagged. So James pressed down harder until it bit and he began to saw.

When he was free, Cook took the knife from James and began cutting away with his one good hand to release the boy.

'What do we do next?' asked James. But the old man just kept sawing and, when he was free, the boy held Cook's hands between his own and they were silent for a moment, bowed like statues in a crypt.

Then they heard something.

'Look,' said Cook, and James stared up at the open doorway at the top of the stairs. Silhouetted in the daylight was a person no taller than the boy's knees. The figure crouched and tried taking a step down, but its foot kicked up into the air. The tiny person regained its balance, quicker than Billy had done, planting a small hand on the floor beside it. It stayed there for a moment, looking down the staircase, and then it hauled itself back up the step and into the doorway. As it turned, James picked up the torch and flashed it up the stairs. He saw a wooden face with painted lips and eyes. As the tiny man looked down, James thought he saw it smile, but he couldn't be sure. Suddenly, he wasn't sure

161

of anything except for the cold, damp air in the cellar. It seemed to have grown fingers that were reaching their way through his skin to his heart.

The marionette gripped the door. Started trying to push it shut.

James took a breath. He thought he could hear Cook shouting, but everything in the dark was soft and muffled, and the cold, chill fingers around his heart were squeezing tighter and tighter, forcing him to breathe faster and faster, making the blood pump louder in his ears.

'It can't reach the handle on the other side,' shouted Cook. 'Hurry, James! Do something.'

Suddenly, James heard the words. He felt Cook shaking his arm and it seemed to set his mind free. He heard himself screaming back at Cook and then he was running up the stairs, the torch in his hand marking out spots for his feet.

The oily top steps glistened. James stepped as carefully and as quickly as he could.

The door began to bang. Opening then shutting. Winking a white line of light as the wooden man tried shutting them up in the darkness again.

James drove through the door with his shoulder and fell through into the hallway, palms burning on the carpet. The torch landed on the floor beside him, the bulb a twist of amber in the daylight.

James heard his heart. And then he was up.

Pulling back the door, he saw the small wooden man lying in a heap, squashed against the white panelling that ran below the balustrade for the main staircase of the house. One of its legs had twisted out of its hip and splintered all the way down the front of its thigh. Its painted eyes gave no indication of any pain. There was no breath or movement in its chest. James could not stop staring. He did not understand what this thing was. He told himself he shouldn't try to.

Cook emerged, panting, at the top of the stairs, blinking in the light. His face was the colour of old newspaper left out in the rain.

'What about the old woman?' he gasped.

James shook his head, and then he picked up the wooden man and flung the thing down into the cellar. It landed on the stone floor, beside Billy, and James shut the door and locked it.

Together the two of them crept down the hallway towards the kitchen. There was no sign of the old woman or Webster.

They walked quietly towards the back door. But they both stopped immediately when they saw her through the kitchen window. She was sitting outside in the garden with her eyes closed, perched on a mahogany chair with a blue velvet seat taken from the set of six in the dining room. Silver hair scraped back. A black shawl draped around her shoulders. She seemed to be in a trance, hands folded in her lap.

'What should we do?' whispered James.

Cook said nothing. He remembered how the old woman had been inside his head. She had crept inside him like a chill and the cold had burned him.

'I'm scared too,' said James and he gripped the old man's hand.

The woman opened her eyes. When she saw them, she rose in one long creaking movement, levering herself up out of the chair. James wheeled round, already imagining himself opening the front door, and dragging Cook with him.

But then they stopped dead.

Because she was standing right there in front of them, the leather pouch around her neck pinched between her bony fingers.

James heard Cook gasp.

27

The old woman allowed herself a smile before dropping her head to one side like an inquisitive bird. Her eyes were black and wet. Like two pebbles plucked from a stream.

'We got a job to do, my loves,' she said and pulled out two chairs from the kitchen table, their feet scraping the linoleum floor. Cook went to sit down, as though he had no choice, but James pulled him gently back. The old woman drummed her fingers on the laminate table-cloth for a moment and then muttered something.

The daylight in the kitchen dimmed slightly.

Whisperings nipped at James's ears.

But he did not listen as he picked up his knees and charged into her, closing his eyes before he looked too deeply into hers. His nose connected with something hard, driving his breath down into his stomach, where it stuck for a moment before flying up out of his mouth as he tumbled forward.

The old woman grunted as she fell with him. Her leather pouch went into orbit around her neck, and then jerked back on its cord and slammed down hard beside her head as she landed on the floor with James on top of her. It split at once, and a stream of seeds and pebbles and tiny bones skittered across the linoleum. She gasped as if dealt a mortal blow. And then her face curdled as she wrapped her arms around the boy.

Her skin smelt of dark lace and roses. Broth on a stove.

James struggled to right himself, but her fingers hooked his thin sweater like brambles. Her lips peeled back. Spit bubbled between worn grey teeth.

His nose was hot. Wet. Blood dripped from it on to the woman's forehead, and ran along the creases and down into her eyes, which she tried blinking clear as she refused to let go of James's sweater.

And then, suddenly, a great force gripped him on either side, jolting him free of the old woman.

James saw muddy boot prints glistening on the kitchen floor as Webster lifted him through the air.

The man dumped him down and stood over the woman who scrabbled backwards, until she came to a stop against the wall, the boy's blood glistening on her face.

He strode towards her and crouched down and wrapped his hands around her throat, making her gasp.

'No,' said James in a frail voice. 'Stop! Please!'

Webster squeezed harder as he looked round ready to roar at James that this was the only way. But the boy was not looking at him. He was kneeling beside Cook who was convulsing on the floor. The old man's blue eyes were screwed down deep into his face, his gums white around his clenched teeth.

The rage inside Webster was still red and balled and hot, and he struggled with it as James laid his hands on Cook, trying to quiet the jerking of the old man's body.

'Please,' said James again to Cook. 'Stop it.'

Webster's hands fell away from the old woman's throat which juddered and crackled as she took in gulps of air.

'Watch her,' said Webster, handing James a knife from the wooden block beside the sink. 'Stick her if she moves, or even says a word.'

And James managed a nod as the knife wobbled in his hand. He looked at the old woman, her chest still heaving.

'What's wrong with him?' James asked quietly as he heard Webster kneeling down beside Cook.

'I think he's having another stroke.'

'We need to call an ambulance.'

'No-ouhhrrhh,' garbled Cook, shaking his head. 'Nooo-ooohh.' His left hand gripped Webster's wrist. 'N-gggot dddiiiss kkk-ime,' he wheezed. Webster nodded.

'I think he wants to be with his wife,' said Webster gently. 'It's his right.'

James turned back to look at Cook who half nodded, lips parted, his tongue winding circles in the air. His eyes bulged, but he managed to flash them at James who saw something hard and certain in them.

'Cook told me something,' he said to Webster. 'Something important. He told me that he was the one who attacked you.'

Webster shook his head. 'No,' he said. 'I would have known.'

'How? How would you have known?' asked James, his voice rising. 'You said you didn't remember anything.'

Webster licked his lips.

'He's too old. Weak. How could *he* have attacked *me*?'

'He did,' pleaded James. 'He told me.' He looked back at the old woman and saw her watching everything intently with her hooded eyes, and he kept his arm raised with the tip of the knife pointing at her.

Webster bent in close to Cook.

'Did you?' he asked quietly. 'Are you the one?' But the old man was already looking beyond him. There was the tiniest of rattles in his throat.

'Tell him,' said James urgently, glancing round. 'Tell Cook you forgive him.'

Webster blinked. Shook his head. 'It's not that easy,' he whispered. He looked down at the swirling red pattern on the linoleum floor. There was an anger swelling in him. Bright and hard. Moving in shapes in the wet of his eyes. The words he wanted did not come, burning up inside him before they could be spoken.

He clasped his trembling hands in front of him.

But his whole body shook.

All that could be heard in the room was Cook's tiny gasping.

'I . . . I deserved it, didn't I?' said Webster quietly. 'I deserved what happened to me.' He looked up at James who was staring straight at him. 'Because of that little girl.'

'No.' James shook his head. 'That's not true.' He could feel the old woman staring. And when he glanced at her again she was watching, entranced, her mouth hanging open. The knife in his hand wavered as he looked back at Webster and felt his own heart cracking. And he shook his head again as if trying to will it to stop breaking apart. 'It wasn't your fault.'

Webster bowed his head and held on to Cook, and James watched the old man's face grow still. And then there was nothing but complete silence into which he seemed to be falling forever.

When Webster realized the old man was gone, he crossed Cook's arms over his chest and shut his eyes. Then he rolled into a ball on the floor and began to sob into the hollow his body had made.

James heard a sound behind him. The old woman was reaching out and scooping up the seeds and pebbles and tiny bones lying around her, whispering to them as she placed them in the palm of her hand.

Her knees clicked as she stood up.

The knife in James's hand wilted and she brushed it aside. She knelt down beside Webster and laid a hand on him, shushing him. Cooing softly to him. Patting his side as though he was an animal lying in a barn in the hay.

'So much for that vicar of yours,' she said, 'and what he told you.'

James looked away and found himself staring at Cook, lying peacefully on the floor, still as a statue on a tomb. His heart clenched tighter and tighter in his chest as he started to panic about something deep down inside him. When he blinked, he tried not to see his mother lying there. But it was hard not to think of her with Cook so still and pale.

'Where's he gone?' he asked quietly. 'Where's my mum? Are they together?'

The old woman turned and looked at him. The lines in her face were decades long, and deep and crusted red where his blood had dried on her. When she opened her fist, James saw the dried seeds and tiny bones and pebbles heaped in her palm.

'There's only nature,' she said. 'The world and our journey through it. We are what we are, part of everything we see around us. Just like these charms, which my mother gave to me and her mother gave to her and I'll give to my granddaughter when my son gets round to giving me one.' She flickered a smile, but then shook her head and clicked her tongue on her teeth. 'The world is full of suffering, my love. And when you leave it that suffering ends because there's nothing.' She nodded at Cook. 'Look how peaceful he is.'

James tried to move. But his bones were heavy, and the tendons and ligaments that kept him strapped together threatened to crack and fall apart.

'I'm so tired,' he said to her. 'Is it because of you?' But the old woman said nothing else. So James just sat there, watching her stroking the ball that was Webster and whispering into his ear.

Eventually, she raised her voice for James to hear too.

'All this running away won't do anyone any good. And I'll tell you why, my loves. Because there is no way of lifting the curse from this poor man,' she said, stroking Webster's hair. 'There's no way of undoing what's been done. I know the history of these things and how they work. And I would know about a cure if there was anything to know.'

James struggled to think. Thoughts came to him in a blur and he spun them into words. And then he crept slowly towards the woman and sat beside her.

'Cook didn't attack him,' he whispered so Webster would not hear. 'We made it up.'

'Well then,' she whispered back, as though playing a game with him. But James shook his head.

'Because of the newspaper,' he said. She watched him as he struggled to piece his thoughts together. 'Because,' and he lowered his voice again so he could barely be heard, 'because he wasn't attacked by any sort of creature at all.'

The old woman smiled.

'Then who attacked him?' she asked. 'Who cut up his shoulders and made him bleed?' James tried to remember what he should say, but his thoughts kept slipping. And the old woman nodded. 'I know the truth of it,' she said. 'I surely do.'

A distant shouting cannoned in the bowels of the house and she asked James to go and open the cellar door for Billy. And the boy did what he was told because it seemed the easiest thing to do. She was right. Running was too tiring now. And thinking everything through was beyond him.

When Billy stumbled up the cellar stairs, he blinked in the daylight and rubbed the swelling along his jaw.

'What's happened?' he growled.

'Cook's dead,' replied James.

When Billy saw the haze in the boy's eyes and knew his ma was all right, he grunted and pushed his way past.

They left Cook lying peacefully in the kitchen, on the linoleum floor, with the sunlight drifting all around him. As the four of them walked across the lawn towards the door in the cedar fence that opened on to the lane, not one of them looked back at the house.

Before leaving, the old woman had made another pot of tea and asked James to drink a mug's worth, and Webster two, saying it would calm them. She poured the rest into a Thermos flask she found in one of the cupboards and stowed it in her red leather bag together with the broken marionette. And then she made sure she had picked up every last seed and pebble and bone before tying her leather pouch shut with a piece of string.

As James stood in the lane, he breathed in the sunlight and listened to the sounds of birds and the whirring of insects. Noticing a flower beside his shoe, he crouched down by the verge and looked it full in the face, recalling dimly that Cook had told him to look for something there.

When he glanced up to ask the woman if she might know what it was, she put her finger to her lips. So

James stood up and waited until a green Vauxhall car came down the lane, driven by Billy, and stopped beside them. Webster climbed into the back seat and sat in silence. And James settled beside him.

As the car drove through the town, James watched the people in the streets and the traffic on the roads. And he thought again of what Cook had told him to do. But it was still unclear. So he leant forward and tapped the old woman on the shoulder.

'Do you know what Cook meant? About the flower? About what to look for?'

But all she did was peer round and shake her head as the indicator started ticking and they turned on to the dual carriageway.

28

James awoke when the car stopped. He peeled his face off the brown plastic seat and squinted in the daylight. Through the window he could see the white torso of a petrol pump and three nozzles plugged into their ports.

The grey underside of the canopy over the forecourt was like a patch of winter sky.

The pump whined as Billy filled the tank. Webster stirred, but did not seem to notice where they were or even recognize James. The boy's eyes were sleepy too and he was about to lay his head back down when he noticed a car parked on the opposite side of the pump. The driver, a middle-aged man with a moustache, was filling up his estate car. Sitting in the back were two teenagers. A boy and a girl.

Both of them were staring at James.

He turned slowly and looked over his shoulder to see if anything might be going on behind him. Nothing. When he turned back round, he saw that the teenage boy had rolled down the car window beside him and was talking to the man with the moustache. The man looked up in the direction of James. He squinted for a moment. Shrugged and shook his head, and looked back at the numbers on his pump.

The teenagers in the back seat just kept staring. And then the girl had an idea and they bunched their heads together.

Billy clicked the petrol cap shut. He wiped his hands on the squares of his dogtooth trousers and then headed for the cashier, peeling off notes from a springy wad.

The man with the moustache left his car to pay too. When he was halfway across the forecourt, one of the doors of the estate car opened. The girl and the boy dropped down on to the black tarmac. They kept low over the few metres between the cars and peered in through the window at James.

He blinked at them. They spoke to each other in muffled voices, nodding until one of them tried the handle of the door.

But it was locked.

When the old woman in the front seat suddenly turned round, they ducked down out of sight.

'How are things, my love?'

James nodded. It was all he could manage. The fog in his head was too thick to think up any words, even though he knew there were lots hidden away inside him. The old woman reached into the red leather bag by her feet in the footwell and drew out the Thermos flask. She unscrewed the white cup on top and then the cap, and filled the cup with hot tea from the flask. Then she leant around and held it out to James.

'It's the last little bit, my love. Be a good boy and finish it up. We've still got a way to go yet.' Steam unwound and disappeared. A bitter smell curdled the air. She lifted up off her seat to get closer to the boy. 'It's OK,' she said. James reached forward. But, as his fingers wrapped around the cup and he tried to take it, the old woman stiffened and did not let go. She was looking into the wing mirror on the driver's side of the car, and in it she could see the reflection of the boy and the girl squatting beside the rear tyre, whispering to each other.

The old woman handed the cup to James, and then let herself quietly out of the car, and walked around to the rear and asked the children to stand up. James watched her talking to the two of them until he felt something warm spreading over his ankle and into his shoe. He looked down. The cup had fallen from his hand into the footwell. He did not remember how it had ended up there. But he knew he had been holding it. When he reached down to pick it up, he discovered it was empty and the tea had soaked into the black fabric making it boggy under his shoes.

Eventually, the old woman returned to the car and shut out the sounds of the forecourt. James watched the boy and the girl return to their own car without saying a word. They did not look at him again.

'All done, my love?' The old woman was smiling and holding out her hand. James nodded and gave her back the empty cup.

When Billy returned, he was holding a newspaper. After starting up the engine, he nosed the car into a parking space on the edge of the forecourt and spoke to the old woman for a long time. When he laid the newspaper down on the plastic island between their seats, James saw his own face staring back at him out of the blocks of black print. He thought he should say something about the picture. But he couldn't find the words.

When he heard the old woman and Billy laughing, he looked up and saw them staring back at him.

'We was wondering what to do with you, boy,' said Billy. 'Now we know. Cash you in. Yoo'se worth a bit of money.' James heard gears clicking round in his head as he looked at them. But his mind was too hazy and it was difficult to understand what was happening.

'He looks a bit too awake to me, Ma,' said Billy.

'I dosed him up good. He'll most likely sleep the rest of the way.'

'If that's what you say.'

'I do.' The old woman fished out her black shawl from beneath her and handed it to James. 'Wrap yerself in this,' she said. James did what he was told and snuggled against the shoulder of the seat. Billy leant round and perched an old herringbone cap on the boy's head, and pulled the front down over his eyes.

'Sweet dreams,' he growled with a smirk.

29

James kept his eyes shut, but the grey mist drifting through him did not swallow him asleep as it had done before. But his thinking was slow. Ungainly. In the odd clear moment his mind quickened, allowing him to consider what was happening and what he should do. But each one of these passed quickly.

Gradually, as the car rattled on, the mist melted away, leaving nothing but blackness inside him, which felt clean and pure and hard. He stared into it for a while, listening to the soft hammer falls of his heart and the gentle washing of his breath, remembering who he was and what was happening to him.

He opened his eyes a crack, peeking out from underneath Billy's cap. The car was old and the leather back of the driver's seat in front of him was scuffed raw. A starry sky filled the windscreen. Billy and his mam were staring right into it.

To his left was Webster, his back to the boy, hands for a pillow.

James sat quietly. Listening to the drone of motorway traffic.

His mind began to make plans.

Ideas came and went.

The car was travelling too fast on the motorway for him to open the door safely. And he did not want to leave Webster behind. He had no pen or paper to write a message and hold it up to the window. Leaping on Billy might cause the car to crash and kill them all.

He was trapped in a box of metal and glass hurtling along at speed.

What the future held he did not know.

'So then,' said Billy, stretching his neck and pushing back into his seat, making the springs creak. 'What'll we tell the police about the boy?'

'Nothing,' said the old woman. 'He'll do the talking.'

'You'll dose him up to say a story?'

'I will. And then some. I'll fix him up with nightmares that'll rot his brain to mulch. The only thing we got to worry about is who hands him in.'

'Me?'

'No.'

'I'll be all right.'

'No. You won't.'

'Then who?'

'I'm thinking about it. But I know the rest of it.'

'You do?'

'Yes. Old man Willshaw is perfect.'

'Willshaw who's soft on kids?'

'Willshaw who's soft on kids. Because if you know it then the whole world knows it. We'll hide the boy in one of the cages he uses for his dogs.' The old woman shifted slightly in her seat. 'Yer da had some business with him.'

'He did?'

'He did. Some business that went bad. That yer da never put straight before he passed away.'

'So we get two birds with one stone.'

'Yes, we do.'

Neither of them spoke for a while after that. James listened to the swish of passing cars. He wanted to scream and hammer on the window, but he didn't. He had to think of something better. But nothing better came to him.

So he waited.

And waited.

Hoping for a chance.

'I need to stop,' said Billy eventually.

James heard the *tick-tock-tick* of the indicator a moment later.

The car slowed as it came off the motorway.

'Put us somewhere away from the rest,' said the old woman.

Billy ran the wheel through his hands, looking for a space on its own in the car park. Out of the glare of the lights.

He chose a spot and slid the car up a slight incline between two white lines, and clicked up the handbrake and killed the engine.

'You'll be all right with them?' he asked his mother.

'Of course I will. They're dosed. I told ya.'

'Right then. Two minutes. Unless I get lucky.' And Billy laughed at his own joke.

'Chance'd be a fine thing,' said the old woman. 'A man only gets to know himself through his children.'

'Is that right?' Billy leant forward. Pointed up at the big moon. 'Well, Ma, once the punters start flocking to our new attraction, and the money's flooding in, I'll be beating off the ladies with a stick. Mebbe you can help me choose the right one?'

'As long as she gives me a granddaughter, you can choose whoever you want.' She lifted the marionette out of the red bag by her feet and sighed, peeling off a curly white splinter the width of a hair from its cracked leg. 'This'll be hers one day and she'll love it the moment she sees it, just like I did.'

When she looked up and saw Billy staring at the wooden man, she reached out and held his hand and squeezed it. 'Little boys and girls are different. It's just how it is. They're all still loved the same.'

James kept his eyes shut as Billy opened the door. And he did not open them even when the door banged shut, making the car rock. He waited, listening to Billy's footsteps fading along the asphalt. But when he looked deep into himself for a plan there was nothing there.

And then the other door opened.

And closed.

He opened his eyes just enough to see through the webbing of his lashes. The old woman was standing beside the car, holding up the wooden man against the night sky and inspecting his damaged leg.

'Webster,' whispered James. 'Webster?'

A turn of the head. A bleary look. The man stared at James as though waiting to be told what to do.

James looked back at the old woman, who was lit by the waxing gibbous moon as it slipped out from behind a grey slab of cloud.

When he was ready, he removed Billy's cap and started to lean forward slowly into the front section of the car, towards the passenger door, his hand outstretched. But she sensed him moving immediately and turned round, so he lunged the rest of the way, banging down the small metal button with his fist.

The lock clunked.

The old woman flung herself at the door and pulled at the handle, but it snapped back out of her hands. James did not wait. He scrambled over the seat to the driver's door and locked that too. The old woman went to each door in turn, but all four of them were locked. She observed James through the glass for some time, the wooden man crooked in her arm, and James was careful not to look at her for too long.

But the old woman did not start to mutter. There was no whisper of her voice in his head or a dark haze unwinding. And then he realised why. Her leather pouch, wrapped around with string, was sitting in the tray between the two front seats. And when he looked up at her she was staring at it too. She smiled, and shrugged her shoulders and looked away, talking softly to the marionette and pointing towards the buildings at the far end of the car park.

A lone figure was emerging through the sliding doors.

Billy was coming back, walking through the sticky orange glow of the car park lights.

A cloud covered up the moon and the interior of the car dimmed. It seemed to cool James's heart too.

He stared at the empty ignition in the beige plastic casing beneath the steering wheel and then looked up at the old woman. She was smiling at him again, shaking her head. He had no plan. No thought at all about what he might do next.

'What now?' he whispered as Webster watched him from the back seat. The man licked his lips. Tried to speak. Then tried again.

'Bra-ke,' he mumbled and then shuddered as if the weight of just one word was too much. James looked at the pedals. 'Bra-ke,' rasped Webster again. James pressed the pedals with his feet, making them clunk.

Suddenly, he looked up.

Billy was running through the half-dark towards them.

'What do you mean?' James shouted at Webster. 'What should I do?'

The cloud lifted. Moonlight streamed into the car.

It shone off the steering wheel.

Caught the handbrake.

And Webster pointed a trembling finger.

James stared at the glint of the silver button and blinked, and then pressed it in and let the handbrake down.

Nothing happened at first.

And then the car began to trickle backwards ever so slowly.

The old woman slapped a hand on the roof of the car and James heard it squeaking as it slipped away. She banged on the windscreen. Shouted. But James turned away, looking out of the rear window, manoeuvring the steering wheel to follow the slight camber of the car park.

The car kept to a slow pace as James guided it, until it started rolling backwards more quickly towards the slip road coming off the motorway.

Billy was sprinting. But he did not seem to get any nearer as the car picked up speed.

A horn blared. An oncoming car, its lights flashing, swerved to avoid a collision as it came up the slip road off the motorway. James kept going, as straight as he could, jiggling the steering wheel as the hiss of motorway traffic became louder. He plugged in his seat belt. Hit the button for the hazard lights. And banged on the horn as the green car slipped backwards on to the motorway.

Cars swerved.

Horns jammed.

Brakes squealed.

And then there was a thump from behind.

James heard the rear lights shatter. The bending of metal.

The shunt of it was like being hit in a dodgem, the force of it centred in his chest and his neck, knocking out his breath and forcing his eyes shut.

He felt the steering wheel shudder, the tyres skidding as the vehicle spun.

And then the rear of the car hit the central crash barrier and everything stopped.

The breathing in James's chest was electric. And he tried not to remember when he'd last felt like this, in that moment when his life had changed forever.

When he opened his eyes, he found himself staring across three lanes of motorway at the hard shoulder on the other side.

He looked right and saw that another car had stopped in the middle of the motorway, facing the wrong way, nose crumpled, its front bumper lying on the road. Plastic orange pieces glowed like embers, scattered over the tarmac.

When he panicked and looked to his left in the direction of the oncoming traffic, James saw cars stopped in their lanes, their headlights glaring at him.

He peeled his hands off the steering wheel. Took off his seat belt. And popped the lock on the driver's door and opened it. But, before stepping out, he checked back, and picked up the small leather pouch in the tray beside him and gripped it hard, wishing himself and Webster somewhere safe. But all he heard was the idling engines from the waiting cars. And James shuddered. For it seemed there was nothing for him to trust or believe in as he staggered out of the car into the road, the pouch gripped hard in his fist, as he kept trying to wish himself and Webster away.

Nobody else in the other cars seemed to know what to do. Or maybe time had somehow stopped for everyone but him. He was shaking, but he managed to come around the car and open Webster's door.

The man half stepped, half fell on to the road.

James noticed the newspaper lying in the front passenger footwell of the car beside the old woman's red leather bag. There he was in his school uniform, staring back, and a photograph of Timpston too. The picture of the village was so small, yet so powerful. And James knew immediately what he had to do. He stopped wishing for anything magical to happen, and hooked his hands into Webster's armpits and dragged him up on to his feet.

He helped Webster over the crash barrier in the centre of the motorway.

They walked across the lanes.

Stumbled down the embankment on the far side.

And disappeared into the night.

30

The two of them found a barn after it seemed they had walked forever under the stars, Webster stumbling and holding on to James. They stripped apart a bale of hay, covering themselves over with golden threads.

Webster slept fitfully, lashing out with his arms. Crying out for people that James did not know. The boy stared silently up at the rafters, trying not to worry about what was going to happen next. Eventually, his hand crept into the pocket of his jeans and curled around the leather pouch, despite not knowing what to say or do.

It was still before sunrise when Webster awoke, and sat up and rubbed the blood back into his face. It was cold and he pulled the straw up around him like a blanket.

'How are you feeling?' asked James.

'Too much champagne,' joked Webster weakly and the boy grinned. Looking out from the barn, all Webster could see was a landscape of moor lit by the moon and it looked like the bare bones of the world. 'Where are we?'

'Somewhere.'

'Do you know where we're going?'

'No.'

'Well, I wouldn't worry,' smiled Webster. 'That's how it is for almost everyone, I reckon.' But his grin faded as he stared at the moon because he could see it was almost full.

James took out the pages from his back pocket. Unfolded them. And set about scanning the handwritten notes in the margins.

'That old woman's wrong,' he said. 'It says here there are other cures we can try. Wolfsbane, which is a plant. Exorcism. Maybe even—'

Webster held up his hand.

'I'm not sure we'll find any of them before tonight, do you? Not out here. This is a place to get lost in, nothing more. It's probably the best place for me.'

'But wha—'

Webster held up his hand again and closed his eyes.

James folded up his pages and balanced them next to him on the hay. He took a deep breath, thinking very carefully about what he had discussed with Cook, before Billy had put them both in the cellar.

'Most people don't believe what Billy and his ma do.'

'I wish they were right.'

'In those pages it says anyone thinking they'll transform into something else on a full moon is just plain . . .' James weighed different words in his mouth until he found the right one. 'Wrong.'

Webster opened his eyes. 'Do you think I'm cuckoo?' he asked. 'Mad?'

'No.'

'Billy and his ma don't either.'

'No, they don't.'

'And what about Cook? You said he was the one who attacked me, so it must be all true.'

'That's what he told me,' said James, nodding, because he did not want to fight.

'So why bring up what it says in those pages then?' asked Webster in an angry voice.

'I don't know. I was just thinking out loud. Wondering about it all. About everything,' shouted James and he thumped the straw. 'Why couldn't you have forgiven Cook?'

Webster hung his head.

'It's a difficult thing to do,' he said. 'That vicar was right. Forgiving's not easy at all. You have to be brave.'

Neither of them said anything for a while. The moonlight seemed to freeze everything. Even their breath.

'I'm sorry I raised my voice,' said Webster.

'I'm sorry too,' James said, reaching across and lifting the pieces of paper off the hay and putting them back in the pocket of his jeans. 'We should start over. Work out what to do next.'

Webster nodded. He got up and walked round the barn and the boy watched him, waiting to hear what he had to say. But Webster did not say anything and eventually he sat back down beside the boy.

'Any ideas?' asked James.

'I thought I might sit here and see what happens next.'

'Isn't that the same as giving up?'

'I don't think so. Not if there's someone else in control of things.' Webster pressed his hands to the earth and motioned to James to do the same. 'Can you feel it?' he asked.

'What?'

'The world turning. Doing what someone must have wanted it to do.'

'Yes,' said James, even though he couldn't, because he knew it was what Webster wanted to hear.

When the man smiled, James smiled back.

Gradually, the moon set and disappeared, and the light began to change and harden into a dark blue. When Webster asked him if he was hungry, James nodded, and Webster told him he would try to find something in the copse they had passed on their way to the barn. Before he left, he told the boy to keep out of sight and watch for anyone coming.

James sat quietly in the twilight, listening to the dawn as it broke. He heard the occasional high-pitched shriek of a fox echoing across the moor, a thin breeze wasting through the gorse. He pressed his hands flat on to the ground either side of him for a second time, and tried to feel the world turning like Webster had done, but again he felt nothing. Even when he held his breath.

He took out the notes, sifting through them until he found the newspaper cutting of himself. And he laid the picture on his lap and stared at it in the briny, early morning light with the moorland panning out in front of the barn, studded with boulders that reared up in the sunrise as the ground caught fire in patches of purple and green and yellow.

When Webster returned with his hands cupped full of berries, he saw that the boy was asleep, the newspaper cutting soft across his knees. He was careful not to wake him as he sat and ate his share, watching the sun rising steadily and warming the land.

When he heard a noise in the distance, he looked up and saw a Land Rover, a long way off, rocking over the mud track that led up to the barn. Webster watched it until he could see who was driving and then stood up.

He looked down at James.

Then back to the Land Rover.

And then back down at the boy.

'Thank you,' he whispered. And then he left quietly, walking on to the moor, and soon he was lost from sight.

June 14th

31

James heard a man's voice shouting at him to wake up. It was his stepfather, the man's face looming and distorting like the reflection in a fairground mirror.

He woke with a start and found himself staring into the soft brown eyes of a man with a weathered face and grey hair who was holding the newspaper cutting between a rough-hewn finger and thumb.

James panicked.

Stood up.

Looked around.

But there was no sign of Webster.

And then he noticed a small portion of tiny wild strawberries and raspberries heaped in the straw near his foot.

The man, who was watching him, held up his hands, and shuffled a few steps back and crouched down again.

'I'm not going to hurt you,' he said gently. 'I'm a farmer. This is my barn. I came here to fetch that trailer.' And he pointed to a small metal trailer standing in the far corner.

James kept looking around, trying to work out where Webster might be. But he already knew, in his heart, what had probably happened as he found himself staring out across the moor.

He bent down and picked up a raspberry, and turned it slowly through his fingers, thinking hard about what he was going to do now.

'You're that missing boy, aren't you?' said the farmer. 'The one in the newspaper.' He held up the cutting.

'Maybe,' said James, staring at the picture of himself in his blazer.

The farmer thought about that as the boy stood before him in his dirty sweater and jeans. And then he folded up the cutting and offered it back.

'It's James though? Isn't it?'

The boy put the cutting in his pocket and nodded.

The farmer sank back on his haunches and rubbed his chin. 'So what am I supposed to do now?' he asked.

James shrugged.

'There's people worried about you. Your stepfather for one. The police. But it seems to me like you might not want to be found.' He pointed out through the doorway at the moor. 'That's as good a place as any to hide yourself in.'

James nodded as he rolled the raspberry back and forth between his fingers, still unsure about what to do next.

'Even so, you won't find what you're looking for out there,' continued the farmer.

'How do you know what I'm looking for?'

But the farmer did not seem to hear. He shifted his feet, and sat down with his legs straight out in front of him and leant back on his arms. The soles of his black wellington boots were worn and scraped and caked with mud.

'When I was about your age, I lost my dear old mum. Cancer. Got a taste for her guts then her bones. And there was no stopping it after that. I said goodbye to her when I was ten. I'm not sure she knew much about it towards the end, but we'd spent a lot of time not saying goodbye when she was still well enough and that probably counted for a lot more. At least that's what I like to think.'

'What happened to you, after she died?' asked James.

'Life went on. And here I am to prove it.' He clicked his tongue. 'I reckon my old mum'd be pretty proud of that.'

James looked down at his hand when he felt something sticky and wet. The raspberry between his fingers

201

had burst, turning their ends red. He crouched down and started rubbing them clean in the straw. And then he stopped suddenly.

'You read about my mum in the paper,' he said.

'Yes, I did. And?'

'Nothing,' said James when his fingers were clean again.

'Well then.' The farmer studied the boy crouched in front of him. And then he looked away. 'I was unhappy for a very long time after she died. The thing was, I couldn't understand who'd flicked the switch inside me.'

'Flicked the switch?'

'Yes. From on to off.'

'You think there's a switch for people?'

The farmer nodded.

'For their happiness. I couldn't think of any better way to explain it back then. Still can't. And now, years later, I know it's true.'

'How?'

'Because all the way through it's been on and then off. On. Off. And the good bits have been things like meeting my wife, having my own children, working my farm and making friends.'

'What about when the switch was off?'

'Well, certain things are my business and not yours. But I can tell you it's a hard life being a farmer and having children, and watching them growing up and being responsible for them.' He looked out across the moor and stared at something James couldn't see. 'I had a grandson once. He almost grew up to be as old as you.' And then he looked at James and smiled. And the boy smiled and nodded back because speaking didn't seem the right thing to do.

'Who is it that flicks the switch?' asked James eventually.

'Who indeed? I'll leave that up to others to work out. People better qualified than me. But I'll tell you this. It tells me how to live. Because when that switch is off I know it'll come on again eventually. And, when it's on, I know to enjoy the moment because it'll be going off again sometime in the future.'

James looked out at the moorland, watching the shadows of clouds sliding over it.

'I know someone who might like to listen to what you're saying.'

'Where are they?'

James kept looking out at the moor. 'Gone,' he said.

The farmer nodded. 'You look like you could do with a wash and a brush-up. And those berries aren't much of anything for a growing boy. If you want to come back with me to the house, I'm sure my wife'll feed you up and see to you. Then you can decide on what you're going to do next.'

'How do I know I can trust you?'

The man pulled out his mobile phone, and leant forward and gave it to the boy.

'I'm not sure how the stupid thing works anyhow half the time. Smartphone they call it.' And he shrugged and shook his head.

James hit a button and the screen glowed. It was eight-fifteen in the morning on June 14th. There was one bar showing for reception. He weighed the phone in his hand. It seemed as though the whole world was waiting for him to speak.

'Do you believe in creatures that only appear on the night of a full moon?' he asked quietly.

The farmer studied him and then let out a long sigh.

'Well, there's a question,' he said, and looked up at the vaulted wooden ceiling of the barn and thought for a while. 'I'm not sure there's enough for me to say either way on that. Enough clues, I mean.' He smoothed back his grey hair with one hand. 'There's a full moon tonight though. So if you're planning on seeing something then I reckon you'd be in luck, if such things are really true.'

32

The kitchen in the farmhouse had bright pine cupboards and a dark slate floor. An old black Rayburn was set into an alcove in one of the whitewashed walls, and James watched the heat wobbling off it as he sipped his tea and ate the breakfast the farmer's wife had cooked for him.

The phone stayed close to his elbow on the table the whole time.

He could see the farmer out in the yard tinkering under the bonnet of a tractor and, after he had finished eating, he went outside and gave the phone back. The man thanked him and put it away in the pocket of his waxed jacket.

'Can I do anything to help?' James asked. 'In return for breakfast.'

The farmer lowered the bonnet and slammed it shut.

'What are you good at?'

'I don't know. I've never really tried this kind of thing before.'

'Follow me.'

He showed James the outbuildings and what needed tidying, and pointed out a hole in the fence, around the chicken coop, that needed repairing. There were the goats and the pigs to feed too. And James decided to help with that. Lugging the feedbags. Filling the troughs. And scattering potato peelings over the grass. The animals came to him without fear and ignored him once they started eating. James watched them until the farmer returned from fixing a gatepost in the yard.

'What are you watching?' he asked.

'Nothing,' said James. The farmer stood beside the boy, elbows resting on the gate, watching the animals too. Chewing. Grooming. Peeing. Gradually, they wandered off to bask in the sun.

The farmer stretched his arms and legs. 'Maybe we've got it all wrong,' he said.

'Maybe.'

'But that's not the point.' James looked up at the farmer. 'The point is how do we put it right if we have?'

The three of them ate a cold lunch of ham and leftovers and pickles and cheese. In the middle of the table sat a dark loaf of rye bread like a stone.

When the farmer's wife asked James about his stepfather, her husband clicked his tongue, saying there was a time and a place for everything, and she nodded and said nothing more. They ate in silence for a while longer until James cleared his throat and told them he knew he had caused a lot of trouble, but did not know what to do about it.

'Going home might be a start,' said the farmer, raising his eyebrows.

'I can't.'

'Why's that?'

'I wouldn't know what to do about things if I went back.'

'Do about what?'

But the boy said nothing. And the farmer and his wife exchanged a look that said everything.

'There's something more important I need to do,' said James.

'What's that?' asked the farmer, slicing an apple into quarters.

'It's a secret.'

'Well, if you need any help then you just ask.'

They ate in silence for a few minutes more and then James decided he should wash up.

As he swished his hands through the warm soapy water, the farmer's wife placed a pile of dirty plates beside him and whispered that her husband had not been this happy for a long time. Not since before their grandson had died. And James whispered back that he was glad he had made a difference in some small way.

When he had finished and put the clean dishes away, James approached the farmer who was sitting on an old chair outside the house, running a rag back and forth through the top and bottom barrels of a Lanber shotgun with a walnut stock.

'Can we go up on to the moor?' he asked.

'Why?'

'I need to see it.'

'Is this to do with your secret?'

'Yes.'

The farmer looked along the Lanber, as though aiming for something only he could see, and then pulled the trigger. It dry fired once and then he tried again, but the trigger jammed halfway with a strange, dull click.

'Well, I'm damned if I know what's wrong with this bloody gun anyway,' he said, leaning the weapon against the wall and wiping his hands on his trouser legs. 'We can go, but I have a condition. That we make a deal of some sort.'

'If I go home afterwards, you mean.'

The farmer shrugged.

'Thinking about it won't do you any harm,' he said.

'OK.'

The farmer clapped his hands together and beamed.

'So what bit of the moor do you want to see?'

'All of it,' said James and the farmer smiled. 'The landmarks anyway. And the tracks and roads across it.'

The farmer looked at him for a while and sucked in his cheeks.

'It can be a dangerous place if you don't know it. Bogs that'll suck you in. Sheer drops that'll snap your ankles or worse. The mist up there can turn you round and round, and slip inside you till it's fogging up your brain.' He took the boy by the shoulders. His eyes burned. 'It's not the place for games.'

They spent the rest of the afternoon in the Land Rover, driving along tracks the farmer knew by heart. James followed them on the Ordnance Survey map across his knees. They stopped a couple of times. Once for the farmer to clear up a stream of tissues and crisp packets hikers had dumped in the heather, and then to check on a ewe, recently shorn, sitting in an awkward position. There was a bite mark on one of its hind legs, which looked new and raw.

'Fox having a go most likely,' said the farmer as he held the sheep steady between his legs. 'A young'un trying its luck. Got a kick for its troubles I expect. We need to keep an eye on that bite, mind.' And the farmer hauled the ewe into a cage in the flatbed of the Land Rover to take it back to the farm.

The other sheep watched. And chewed. And went back to their grazing as James and the farmer left.

When they returned to the farmhouse, the sun was setting and the sky was red and bloody.

'Useful trip?' asked the farmer. James nodded his head. 'But you're still not going to say why?'

'No.'

'And what about our deal?'

'I'm thinking about it,' said the boy.

The farmer leant in close and listened.

'Yep, I think I can hear the cogs,' he said and smiled.

They ate supper and talked about the day. It seemed to James the three of them were completely safe from the world outside in the warm rosy glow of the kitchen as the windows slowly darkened around them. The farmer laughed and told stories, and his wife scolded him for drinking too much red wine. James was polite and offered up all the conversation he could, telling them he could not imagine anywhere he'd rather be. But deep down he was thinking about later and what he was going to do. The farmer shot him the odd glance, but James kept his secret safe until he went to bed.

He lay on top of his covers, still dressed, listening to the house go quiet after the farmer and his wife had turned out the lights and gone to bed. When he saw the full moon through the gap in the curtains, a thin sweat broke out over his brow, but he wiped it away. Swinging round his feet and planting them on the floor, his legs felt too soft to take his weight. His breath was lean and smoky. He told himself not to be scared.

Sitting on the bed, he stared at the old woman's leather pouch, which he'd placed on the bedside table, and thought carefully about the things he'd seen her do. And then he took out the pages from the pocket of his jeans, leafing through them until he found the note he was looking for, and read it and reread it in the moonlight. According to a German legend, rye bread protected people from being attacked. James looked out of the window at the moon and kept on looking until he had convinced himself that he did not need such a thing to be true. And then he put the notes back into his pocket and let himself out of his room. The last thing he saw before closing the door was the leather pouch sitting on the table.

From the kitchen dresser he took a small black torch that he had noticed earlier when putting the dishes away and picked up the Ordnance Survey map he had left on a chair. As he made for the back door, he stopped and stood quite still when the full moon slipped free from its covering of cloud and began frosting everything in the kitchen with a cold, iron light. It seemed to chill his heart. And even the hope within it.

211

He turned back round. In the pantry he found the rye bread they had eaten at lunchtime in the bread bin. He weighed the quarter loaf in his hands, listening to the thoughts in his head. And then he tucked the bread under his arm.

He left the farmhouse and walked across the yard to one of the barns. The night was thin and grainy in the bright moonlight, and it pulled at the corners of everything he could see. Beneath his feet the hard mud looked like concrete.

He had noticed the old bicycle in the barn earlier in the day. The map and the rye bread went into the basket on the front and then he picked the bicycle off the wall and wheeled it out into the night.

He rode it slowly out of the yard, careful not to make too much noise.

After he had gone far enough, James began to pedal harder down the track, out towards the heart of the moor.

33

It did not take long for the night to swallow him whole. There was no light on the bicycle and no way of fixing the torch to the handlebars, so James tucked it into an armpit. But this was uncomfortable and the beam was pitiful. So he turned it off and threw it into the basket on the front, and pedalled on through the moonlight that ebbed and flowed as clouds moved, and the world turned, and the moon rose up steadily through the sky.

After a couple of miles, he stopped. Listened. But there was nothing but the swish of his own blood in his ears. It was as though he was standing at the bottom of a lifeless ocean. Or even on the moon itself.

'Webster!' His voice cannoned around the rocks and then sank into the dark patches of heather and gorse. 'Webster! Where are you?' But nobody shouted back to him.

He clicked on the torch again and consulted the map. He decided to stay on the track he had taken because he knew it would rise up eventually and give him a better vantage point across the moor.

The dirt on the track muttered as he rode over it, crackling and spitting. Small rocks squirted out from under his tyres without warning and sent him skidding for a second, until he righted himself and kept on going. Occasionally, he stopped and listened, looking all around for anything moving on the moorland below him. But it was difficult to see clearly with the moon muted by the clouds, which shone iron and silver and creamy grey as they swept across it.

When James reached the top of the hill, he stopped and studied the map again. Further on, the track split and he decided he should take the left fork, which would take him out towards the stream he had seen during the day. He told himself that every living thing needed water.

Five minutes or so after the fork, James saw something off the track that did not look right and he stopped. Laying the bicycle down, he walked on, the torch lighting spots in the gorse for his feet.

He paused when he saw it.

The hairs on the back of his neck fizzed as he stood listening, waiting, until he was satisfied he was alone, and then he shone the torch over the body of the dead sheep in front of him, its shorn body glassy and smooth in the beam.

It was lying in the springy heather, as though washed up on a beach of weed. Its throat was a black gaping maw, which became red and bloody in the beam of the torch. James shone the light into the dead creature's face. Bulbous pinks and blacks for eyes, like marbles too big for the sockets. Eyelashes in rows like tiny bones.

The ground around the sheep was spattered with blood. James decided it must have been killed where it lay because there was no trail of blood that he could see and no sign of the animal having been dragged through the heather. He reached out and touched the creature's bony shoulders. The sheep was lukewarm. A shiver ran through him and James turned off the torch.

He crouched down and remained still for a long time, listening to the dark. But the only thing he heard was the hum of the moon and the stars, and the drum of his heart in the soles of his feet.

When his legs grew numb, he stood up to let the blood back into them. Then, in the quiet, he walked back to the bicycle and carried on down the track, ignoring one half of all the thoughts in his head.

Eventually, James heard the water below him, its distant musical notes.

He stopped.

Laid the bicycle on the ground.

And walked to the edge of the track.

The stream cut a black winding groove in the moor and he looked along it from above, following it first to the left, all the way to the horizon of stars, and then to the right.

'Webster! Webster, it's me, James.'

His voice echoed out over the dark landscape and faded into nothing.

He looked at his watch. It had been two hours since he had set out from the farmhouse. The night was more than half gone. As he turned to pick up the bike, he saw something moving on the plain below.

The silhouette of a figure.

Hunched over.

Following the line of the stream.

The boy crouched down and watched the shape until he lost sight of it behind what he thought must be a set of boulders that blipped in the dark as he stared at them. He waited for the figure to reappear, but it did not.

James turned on the torch and began to make his way down on to the moor below, picking his way between rocks and bracken. After a moment, he stopped and turned around and went back to the bicycle. He bent down and ripped a fistful of rye bread out of the loaf in the basket, and held it in his hand and stared at it. And then he hurled it away as hard as he could into the dark, and closed his eyes and whispered to himself

216

that there was nothing to be afraid of at all. Then he walked back down on to the moor.

He followed a rabbit run, which took him some of the way, until it dwindled into nothing.

As he descended, James lost sight of the stream. But he could still hear it so he navigated his way by following the sound. Gradually, the ground turned damp and sucked at his black shoes, making it harder to walk. Cold water seeped through and soaked his socks, turning them coarse and heavy.

Suddenly, the ground gave way and his front foot plunged knee-deep into a bog. He cried out as his arms windmilled, trying to keep him upright, and the torch flew from his hand and landed on the ground, lighting up a small relief of bracken stalks and stones. The muck sucked greedily at James's leg as he tried to pull it free, but then his other leg began to sink too as it took more of his weight.

He allowed himself to fall on to his front, and then stretched out his arms and grabbed at the tough bed of heather growing round him. The short roots tore then snapped. Clumps of soft green came away in his hands. As he scrabbled for more, his fingers found a rock, embedded in the soil, around which he clasped both hands. He hauled. Strained. And the rock held his weight as he pulled himself out of the bog and kicked his legs free. When he was clear of the mud, he lay panting

217

on the ground, staring up at the stars that winked back at him, until he was ready to stand up.

The stream was close by and it was impossible to hear anything else but the suck and run of the water. James picked the torch out of the bracken and wove his way carefully towards the bank, his wet feet rubbing inside his shoes.

When he played the light from the torch across the water's surface, he saw the brown backs of stones and white eddies circling above them. He sat with his legs hanging off the bank and let the stream lick the mud from the soles of his shoes. Then he followed the water towards the set of boulders he had seen from the track.

Drawing closer, James covered the torch with his hand, making his fist glow a phantom red, and allowing himself only the thinnest of light to walk by. He neared the boulders, veering away from the stream, listening for anything moving or breathing.

When he thought he heard footsteps behind him, he whirled round. But there was no one there.

'Webster?' he said softly. But there was no answer.

Cloud curdled over the moon, culling the light around him. James rotated the torch methodically. Eyes sharp. Chest as taut as a drum. And then he saw it.

A figure.

Flitting through the beam.

The black shape of it.

Nothing more.

James flashed the torch around him, trying to pick it up again.

'I saw you!' he shouted. 'Webster, I saw you. There's nothing to be afraid of. It's me, James. Your friend.'

The torch's beam wobbled as his hand shook.

And then a low growl uncoiled around him.

'Webster?' said the boy softly. 'It's not true. None of it is.' But the growling grew. It did not sound human at all, like something drawn from a distant time.

James turned off the torch and the night engulfed him.

There was a dark shape standing off to his right. Its outline seemed taller than Webster had ever been. Maybe he was standing on a rock? James's heart wavered. The constant growling seemed to suck up his courage, turning it thin and watery inside him.

He took a step towards the shape and a loud howl unfurled into the sky. When he heard footsteps, he brought up the torch and pressed in the rubber button as a figure loomed up in front of him and lashed out, catching his arm, as it leapt past.

The torch went flying, end over end . . .

. . . but all James saw was a flash of white pain behind his eyes. As soon as his right hand started to throb, he held it up and saw two fingers twisted out of their knuckles.

The boy gasped. Wet blurred his eyes. He stumbled forward, looking for the torch, but he could not see its light anywhere. A growl behind hurried him on and he came up against the set of large boulders.

A narrow mouth running diagonally between the rocks was just wide enough. James felt into the dark with his good hand and then slid forward through the gap.

Feet thundered.

The turf shook.

And James squeezed himself tighter and tighter to try and slip through.

He cried out as a great weight barrelled into him from behind and a sharp pain raked his shoulders. The force knocked him through the opening and he landed in a heap on the floor of a small cave bounded on all sides by the boulders.

Something scrabbled at the narrow entrance and then stopped.

James heard the pitter-patter of feet above him. Growling dropped down through the tiny cracks in the stone and filled the cave until the boy buried his head in his arms and began to sob. In the dark, questions flashed and spun. But he had no answers for any of them.

When he finally looked up and listened again, the growling had gone. The night seemed perfectly still. He was alone except for the skeleton of some small animal, which gleamed in the moonlight slanting through the tiny gaps between the boulders. The pain in his two crooked fingers was ugly and dull. A fire licked down his shoulders. Stretching round, he saw that his sweater was ripped and raggedy, with the skin beneath it black and sticky.

James wondered what it was that could have done such a thing. He sat thinking about it for a very long time. But no true answer came to him. He was not sure what to believe about what had happened. Slowly, his body grew colder and he started to shiver. It became harder to think things through as the pain in his shoulders spread like a tangle of roses growing up over his back, catching hold with their tiny barbs. When he closed his eyes, he saw his mother and Cook, and shouted at them, asking why they had left him here in this world on his own. But they said nothing and, as soon as James could no longer stand their mute, staring faces, he opened his eyes and tried to breathe away the pain. He could not imagine anyone feeling more alone than him, trapped in a prison made of cold stone and moonlight.

Every time he thought about leaving, he heard a noise outside and shrank back from the opening into a ball, wondering if it might be Webster, the one person in the world who had promised never to hurt him and whom he had trusted with all his heart.

*   *   *

221

James stayed in the hollow until dawn, the moonlight ebbing and flowing around him.

In the clean, early morning light he hauled himself back through the narrow opening in the rocks and stood looking over the moor, which was wet and gleaming, as if a tide had washed over it and rubbed it clean for the new day.

When he found the torch lying face down in the heather, the wire in the bulb glowing pale orange, he switched it off and put it in his pocket. Then he stumbled slowly back to the track, and picked up the bicycle and wheeled it beside him. His shoulders felt lumpy and stiff, and hurt with every step. His crooked fingers were numb. It was slow going and he knew it would take a long time to get back to the farmhouse.

When he saw a bird appear in the sky, wheeling effortlessly above him in the blue, he gawped like a much younger child, wishing he had its wings.

After a while, James saw the farmer's Land Rover appearing over the skyline, bumping towards him along the track. James stopped and waited for it to reach him. He did not know what he was going to say, but he remembered how safe he had felt with the farmer and his wife in the kitchen eating supper the night before, and willed the vehicle on faster towards him.

Sky slipped over the windscreen as the vehicle drew closer. When it stopped beside him, James began to shake. He leant against the side of the Land Rover and saw a pair of red-rimmed eyes staring back from the wing mirror. His face was so white it was grey and it shone with a sickly, waxy sheen. The night was still inside him and he threw it up on to the stones at his feet. A crow scudded down into the heather beside the track and cawed as James heard the driver's door open.

Footsteps walked round the front of the vehicle and stopped beside him.

'Yoo'se in a state, boy,' said a voice.

It was not the farmer.

James was looking up into the face of Billy.

June 15th

34

James tried to run, but his back was too sore. His legs and arms were wooden. So Billy caught him easily, and lifted him up and manhandled him into the cab of the Land Rover.

He was too tired to move and lay curled up on his side against the seat, listening, as Billy threw the bicycle into the flatbed. Then the man came round and got into the cab, and sat quietly beside him for a moment while he caught his breath.

'Where's Webster?' he asked.

'I don't know,' said James. 'I don't know anything.' Tears nipped at the edges of his eyes, making him blink, and he said nothing more.

Billy lit up a cigarette, and opened the window and blew the smoke out into the early morning sunshine. Picking a strand of tobacco from his tongue, he rolled it between his fingers and flicked it away.

'Well, I'm not sure it matters now anyway.'

He started the engine and turned the Land Rover round. On the bumpy journey back to the farmhouse, James tried to understand what Billy had meant. But his mind kept slipping because of the pain in his shoulders and the throbbing in his fingers. His thoughts were nothing more than air that drifted up and out of him across the moor.

When they reached the farmhouse, Billy parked next to a sky-blue Ford estate, and helped the boy out of the Land Rover and over the muddy yard. They opened the door and went into the kitchen where the old woman was sitting at the pine table, a white mug in her hands, waiting, as James had expected her to be. Lying in front of her was her leather pouch. She set down the mug, and picked up the pouch and held it in her palm for James to see.

'Every charm and talisman in here is mine and a part of me,' she said to him. 'They know that. We belong to each other.'

She asked Billy to bring the boy over to her as she placed the leather pouch in the pocket of her skirt.

'Where's the farmer and his wife?' asked James in a tiny, cracked voice. The old woman ignored him and inspected the marks on his shoulders beneath his ripped and ragged sweater, and then asked how he had come by them.

James told her nothing.

'They're both safe,' she said. 'Asleep upstairs.' Then she waited for James to tell her what she wanted to know.

'I don't know how it happened,' he said.

'What do you think happened?'

He shook his head.

'I don't know.'

'I think I do. It's all written here, with blood for ink.'

She made James sit down beside the warm stove, and then took a pair of scissors and cut away carefully at his sweater until she could peel it off him. His bony white shoulders were covered in dark-red blood.

The old woman gave him a cup of sweet black tea to drink as she washed his wounds tenderly, whispering to him all the time. When he asked again about the farmer and his wife, the old woman shushed him, her fingers working delicately over his skin until all the pain had vanished, leaving him warm and woozy, as though he had slipped loose from the real world into a dream, unable to remember quite when or how it had happened.

'I thought you were gone forever,' he said, staring into the old woman's eyes where the grey colours looked as soft as wool. He reached out with his good hand and clung on to her fingers as if never, ever wanting to let go. 'But you were watching all along, Mum, weren't you? So you know he hates me now. Hits me. Because all he had left after the car accident was me and he can't do anything about it, and neither can I. We're all we've got.' James edged closer to the old woman on the seat of his chair. 'What's it like, Mum? What's it like where you are? Is it safe?'

When he asked again, the old woman shushed him until he sat back in his chair. Out of the half-thinking and broken thoughts, James suddenly announced that the old woman must have been a good mother to Billy, kind and gentle, just like his mother had been to him when she had been alive. The old woman nodded and then glanced at Billy, and something wordless passed between them in a smile.

Then, as gently as she could, she took hold of James's two dislocated fingers and snapped them back into their joints one after the other. And, although it was no more painful for him than watching it happen to someone else, he began to remember where he was and what had happened to him on the moor.

After fixing his hand, the old woman prepared a poultice. She selected various herbs, which looked to have been freshly picked, from her pockets, and dropped them into a black casserole dish she had found in a cupboard and boiled them gently on the stove. A sweet, oaty smell swelled in the room and fogged the windows.

She soaked a dishcloth in the thin water then laid it over James's wounds and left it there.

All three of them sat in silence until the old woman removed the poultice, dressed the wounds and informed Billy they could leave.

Billy stood up. Helped the half-naked boy from his chair and led him towards the door.

When the old woman picked up a knife from the drying rack beside the sink and turned to go upstairs, James halted, despite Billy trying to push him on.

'I won't go with you if anything happens to them,' he said. But Billy just started dragging him towards the door. And James yelled and grabbed at the door frame and clung on. 'If you hurt them then I'll know there's something good in the world. Something really good!'

The old woman motioned to Billy and he stopped trying to pull the boy out through the doorway.

'Why would you think that, my love?' she asked.

James wiped his eyes and coughed to clear his throat. He drew in a breath and shuddered. 'Because how else could there be something as horrible and as evil as you?' he said.

When she waved her hand, Billy wrenched James out through the doorway into the yard despite his crying.

She stood at the bottom of the stairs, watching the boy being dragged towards the sky-blue Ford. Then she turned and went upstairs, the leather pouch clinking in her skirt pocket.

The farmer and his wife were lying on the crimson eiderdown covering their bed. Dressed in their clothes. Fast asleep. Chests rising and falling. The old woman's eyes flicked back and forth between their soft white necks and the knife in her hand.

She could hear James outside, screaming and shouting, and Billy cursing out loud. As the noise grew louder, she walked to the half-open window and looked down at James, who was clinging on to the car door as Billy tried to shove him inside. The more he kicked out, determined not to go in, the angrier and rougher Billy became until he raised his arm to strike the boy.

'No!' she cried out. The two of them stopped and looked up, blinking in the sunlight at her. 'We don't want to go hurting him! You're not yer da!'

Billy slapped the top of the car. 'He says he won't go in! How else is he gonna learn to do what he's told?'

The old woman stared down at them.

Clouds drifted.

A bird drummed past the window.

Her knees creaked.

'They're going to be all right,' she shouted eventually. 'As long as you get in the car. You're gonna have to trust us.' And with that she walked away from the window and back to the bed. After stowing the knife in her waistband, she leant over the sleeping couple and blew into her fists, opening one each over the face of the farmer and his wife, and waited for their eyes to flicker open.

'We're leaving now,' she said to them. 'So you best come and wave us off.'

Downstairs, in the kitchen, she nodded approvingly when she saw James sitting in the back seat of the car, watching the house. Billy was waiting in the driver's seat, drumming the steering wheel with his thumbs. When she saw the farmer's Lanber shotgun with the walnut stock resting against the wall in the porch, she picked it up. And then she turned to the farmer who was standing with his wife, waiting to be told what to do.

'Do you have any cartridges for this?'

The farmer disappeared into the boot room beside the kitchen, returning with a box of cartridges that he handed to her.

'Now you make sure and wave us off, then you can go back to doing whatever you was busy on.'

She walked out into the yard. Climbed into the passenger seat of the Ford, and smiled at the little wooden man sitting in the footwell by her feet and leant down and whispered something. Then she handed the shotgun and cartridges to Billy.

'What do we need these for?'

'We need to go up on to the moor.'

'Why?' asked Billy. 'We've got the boy.'

The old woman sat still and looked out at the moorland.

'Because we have to if we want to keep him,' she said, staring out through the windscreen.

Billy hesitated, and then he turned the key in the ignition and the engine came to life. As the car began to move, the old woman turned and waved at the farmer and his wife. But James didn't wave. He just watched them, telling himself to try and keep remembering their smiling faces.

When the car came out of the yard, it stopped beside the track, leading away from the lane that would take them back to the main road.

'You're sure?' Billy asked her.

'Yes.'

'Do you know where he is?'

'I will. Take the track on to the moor.' The old woman looked back at James slumped in the seat with his head still turned, staring back at the farmer and his wife. 'They'll be OK,' she said to him. 'But they won't remember you. So you best forget them too. We made a bargain, remember? So you be good now. You wouldn't want to go back on yer word now, would you?'

And then she turned round and settled back in her seat, and closed her eyes.

James sat, looking out of the window, his mind only half working as the pain in his shoulders lurked just below the surface of him. He felt leaden and sore, a lump of a boy, as the car moved. Finally, he managed to lean forward, swallowing sharply as the wounds on his shoulders creaked.

'Thank you,' he said quietly before sitting back in the seat and breathing away the pain as well as he could. But all the time he kept telling himself he would run away as soon as he had enough strength, escaping again just like he and Webster had done before. Whenever the opportunity arose.

As the car bumped along the track, he noticed a black dot high above them in the sky. A bird of some sort. Circling slowly. Growing larger in the blue. As it dropped lower and lower, he saw it was a crow, its black fingers spread at the ends of its wings. It swooped past and landed in the scrub ahead of them, and hopped through the heather, stopping on the track in front of the car.

Billy braked.

The engine throbbed.

A wind rocked the car.

The bird stared up at them as the old woman began muttering under her breath, and it seemed to James the crow was joining in with her, talking too.

As soon as she stopped, it launched itself into the air, catching the wind and spiralling higher and higher, until James lost sight of it against the sun.

It was five minutes before the old woman said anything, her shoulders twitching, her head moving slowly back and forth.

'Straight ahead,' she whispered to Billy.

35

Billy looked back once more at the sky-blue Ford parked on the track before the ground swallowed him up. He reckoned he must have walked more than half a mile after following the rabbit run over the scrub before reaching the gully. The backs of his heels were beginning to rub raw. His boots were not meant for this type of walking.

As he trod carefully down, below the level of the moor, the air began to cool. Instead of gorse and heather to his right, there was just a wall of hard brown rock. Billy patted it with the flat of his hand, as though calming the spirit of a horse, and then continued on down the trail, such as it was, the rock face guiding him.

Loose stones ran ahead of him, chattering. Some falling over the edge into the tea-coloured river below.

Billy peered to his left all the way down. The water was running hard and fast, a yellowish curd riding the surface, clinging to the edges of rocks.

The noise of the water rose with the spray and he heard nothing else as he walked carefully down.

When he reached the bottom, he followed the river's flow, slowing when he saw a pool ahead of him, dark and oily, with currents circling the surface.

He stopped when he saw the dead sheep in front of him, lying on a flat section of rock overhanging the pool, its head looking down at the water. There was no blood. Just scree pooled nearby. He looked up at the sheer rock face above, all the way to the blue sky at the top, wondering what might have caused the creature to fall. It could have been an accident. Or something might have scared the animal over the edge.

Billy moved warily as he passed it, its pink tongue hanging from the corner of its mouth.

Rounding a sharp bend, just past the pool, he stopped again and held his breath.

Webster was crouched on a bed of flat rock by the water's edge. Semi-naked, his trousers ripped and torn around his ankles. His wet black hair was scraped back and glistening, and there were ugly grey scars on his shoulders.

Billy crept slowly, letting the water cover the sound of his footsteps.

But Webster seemed to hear him anyway and looked up.

Quickly, Billy raised the gun.

And fired.

36

James listened. The old woman listened. But there was only the echo of the single gunshot rolling over the moor until it was gone, wasted into the wind.

'A clean kill then,' she said, smiling, as if trying to soften the blow. James wanted to fling open the door and run, but the old woman's smile forced him to shrink deeper into the seat and close his eyes. In the dark he saw the face of Webster staring back at him. As though the man was trapped inside his head forever. James whispered to him, telling him he was safe now and could never be harmed again by anything or anyone. All the anger and disappointment at what Webster had done was nowhere to be found. Maybe it was spent. Or maybe it was still raging somewhere out of sight. James didn't know. All he could do in that cold, hard moment as the wind whistled round the car was to sob for the man who had been his friend, his ally against the pain in the world.

He opened his eyes and wiped the wet in them when he heard Billy's boots clumping down the track. The old woman leant across and opened the driver's door, and Billy sat down behind the wheel. In one hand was the Lanber shotgun. In the other was a heart. Slippery and glistening. It had been rinsed somewhere in water.

'This what you wanted?'

The old woman nodded.

'You should have wrapped it in something soft, like bracken,' she said before Billy could complain about carrying it back.

She lifted the heart carefully out of his hand and wrapped it in her black shawl, then bound it up inside a white supermarket bag which had been scrunched in a ball beside the wooden mannequin in the footwell.

The heart sat on her lap.

Like shopping, James thought.

Billy wiped his hands on a chamois leather, which he stuffed back into the doorwell beside him, and then started up the Ford. He drove back along the track and then out on to the lane to join a road.

When he reached a junction, the car turned left and gradually the road became larger and wider.

Eventually, they turned on to a slip road which led them down to a motorway.

No one spoke for the whole journey back to the fair.

37

It was almost dark when the car pulled up in the traveller camp. James recognized Billy's caravan, its bright green writing electric in the headlights, but not the place in which it was standing, with concrete blocks wedged behind the wheels.

The fair had moved on since he had tried to bargain for his gold. Now it was pitched in the field adjoining the one that Billy had stopped in, outside a different town that shimmered orange in the near distance, pumping thumping music into the night sky that seemed to make the stars sparkle.

James had no idea where he was after losing track of the road signs as the roads narrowed and the day wound round to dusk. He thought he could smell the sea, but he couldn't be sure.

A toilet flushed somewhere.

A dog barked.

Billy took James by the arm and led him across the dark field to another smaller clearing, away from the knot of caravans and the fairground. There they found an old wagon cage on wheels, which was wooden, except for the black metal bars down one side. It looked old and brittle in the moonlight. There were washed-out patterns in red and green on the thin panels above and below the bars. The rest of it was a weather-blistered blue.

Without saying a word, Billy dragged James up a set of white painted steps, opened the steel door and pushed the boy inside.

The door slammed shut.

A lock turned.

And James rushed back to the door.

But there was no handle on the inside.

And the steel felt solid and strong when he pressed his hands against it.

He ran across the wooden floor to the bars and looked out between them. Billy was walking away to the left, back towards the caravans standing out of sight, and he soon disappeared into the dark. James could still hear the fairground, even though he couldn't see it, and pushed his face as far as he could into the gap between two cold bars and yelled.

Laughter in the distance.

A faint hubbub.

The odd delighted scream keening.

James shouted until he was hoarse.

But no one came.

Boots clumped up the steps. A key clicked round in the lock.

The steel door opened and Billy trudged into the dim-lit wagon with a bucket which he set down in a corner on the bare wooden floor. He drew out a metal bowl full of something hot and steaming from the bucket, and then reached back in, retrieving a wooden cup which he placed on the floor. Billy took a wooden spoon out of his back trouser pocket and held out the bowl.

'Ma says to eat this broth. It'll help you feel better.'

'I'm not hungry.'

'She'll be along in a minute. You can tell her yerself if you want.' Billy put the bowl on the floor beside the cup and slid the spoon into the steaming mixture. 'The cup's for water. Just tip it up and drink. It won't run out. The bucket's for yer business.'

He closed the door behind him.

The key turned in the lock again.

Footsteps padded away.

James picked up the bowl of broth and sniffed it. Hedgerows and mud. He swirled the spoon and pearl barley bobbed in the liquid. He was hungry enough to try it. It tasted slick and sweet and wholesome, and he ate as much as he was able.

When he had finished, he picked up the wooden cup. It was empty, but when James tipped it up, as Billy had told him to do, water ran up over the lip and on to the floor. When he looked again, the cup was empty. He tipped it up a few more times and, each time, water appeared at the lip. Yet, every time afterwards, the cup was empty. The boy stared at the wooden bottom and shook his head because he did not understand it.

He wished he had not eaten the broth.

When the door opened again, it was the old woman who stepped through into the wagon. Billy stood behind her, waiting on the white steps, his outline clear in the bright moonlight.

She glanced into the almost-empty bowl.

'Good boy,' she said, nodding.

After inspecting the wounds on James's shoulders, she left the dressings off, folding them up and putting them in her skirt pocket.

'There's stories that the moon can heal creatures like you,' she said, looking up at the sky through the bars. 'You should bathe tonight in the waning moonlight. Draw as much strength from it as you can.'

'Creatures like me?' whispered James.

And the old woman shone back a smile and nodded, and picked up the metal bowl and the spoon, and left.

Before he closed the door, Billy threw in a thin stripy mattress that flopped on to the floor like a dead fish. Two red blankets landed on top of it.

James sat alone on the dirty mattress and looked up at the moon. His shoulders and his neck were sore, and he turned to let the moonlight fall on them. But it seemed to make no difference. Eventually, he lay on his side, staring at the wooden wall opposite, trying not to think about anything except for who he was.

When he rolled over, he felt something uncomfortable in the front pocket of his jeans. It was the small black torch he had taken from the farmer's kitchen. He pressed in the rubber button, and the light roared into the dark and lifted his heart. He started remembering everything he could about the farmer and his wife, and all the good in their faces, flashing the light around the walls of the wagon to try and chase away the dark. But the night wouldn't leave, only shrinking back and then creeping forward again as soon as he moved the beam.

The wagon was smaller than his bedroom in Timpston. For the first time since leaving home he wished himself back in his bed, safe under the covers. But then his stepfather's face loomed up inside him and made him shudder, and he stared into the shaky pool of light on the wall until his hand had stopped trembling.

247

After turning off the torch to save the batteries, and hiding it under the mattress, he lay down and fell asleep to the distant sounds of the fair. He conjured himself into a long, slow dream wherein the world had ended and he was the only person left wandering through an ashen waste with no one left to speak to. All he could do was keep walking, hoping to find some way out of the desolate wasteland where the silence was so loud it hurt his ears and the blood in his bones.

June 16th

38

James awoke as soon as the door opened. The daylight and the quiet shocked him as he stared at the green field in front of the wagon, steaming gently in the early morning sun. A blackbird took fright at something, trilling as it strobed past the black metal bars, its shadow ticking through the golden bands of sunlight lying evenly spaced on the wooden floor. He righted himself on the mattress and huddled the blankets closer as the old woman walked towards him.

Billy waited on the steps like before as she inspected the boy's wounds, sighing her disappointment when she saw they had not healed.

'Some of these stories are so old,' she said, 'that no one really knows any more what's true and what en't.' She tapped her chin. Tugged at the hairs sprouting from one of her ears. 'A child like you is a very rare thing,' she said, smiling. 'Valuable too.' And she looked over at Billy who smiled back. 'At least we'll have new stories to tell now,' she continued, 'and I'll make sure they won't get lost like before.' She waved her hand at Billy and he threw her an old black sweater which she caught in one bony hand. It was the one James had been wearing on the moor. But the holes in the back had been stitched up and the whole thing had been washed clean.

She applied new dressings to his wounds, and then rolled the sweater carefully down over James's head and torso, trying not to hurt him.

When she stood up, James hooked his hand around her arm to stop her leaving.

'Am I really different now?' he asked. 'Am I really cursed?' The old woman nodded. 'But I don't feel different. Nothing's changed inside.'

'It will. The next full moon will make it happen.'

'I never saw Webster on the moor.'

The old woman smiled. 'He saw you though, didn't he?' she said.

'I mean I never saw what he was. If he was really what you said.'

'Would he have done this to you if he wasn't?'

When she turned to go, he tugged on her arm again, pulling her back.

'Webster was a soldier. He's seen terrible things which upset him. Changed him. I think he might have believed he was cursed because that's what you told him.'

'And why would he have believed that, my love?'

James felt himself shaking. 'Because . . .' He licked his lips and took a breath. 'Because he might have been confused about a lot of things.'

But the old woman just smiled.

'Is that what you really think?' She pointed at his shoulders. 'Would he really have done that to you if he was only a man?'

James blinked back at her, remembering how Webster had promised never to hurt him. And then he looked down at the wooden floor. But there were no answers there.

'I don't know,' he said, shaking his head. 'I can't say I know anything for sure.'

The old woman laughed. A dry, brittle sound.

And then she walked away.

Out of the wagon.

Down the steps.

And across the dewy, steaming grass.

Billy locked the door. And then he unhitched a pair of wooden shutters on the outside of the wagon at either end of the bars and began pulling across the one on the left.

'Ma says the daylight's not for someone like you no more. You best forget about it. Like the world out there's gonna forget about you too. Yoo'se a whole different person now.'

'The world won't forget about me. My picture's in the paper.'

Billy shrugged.

'You en't the only news. Things move on. And what we got planned means the world en't never gonna see you. Not like this anyway.'

'What are you going to do with me?'

'Work you. For a while. And then who knows after that? Depends on you.' Billy thought about something as he brought round the left-hand shutter to the middle of the bars. Then he smiled and stood looking at James. 'See, what you got is a gift. One you can give to someone on a full moon. Now people'll pay once to see a freak and be scared. But the next time around they'll be expecting something more. Double the thrill for double the money. And that's where you come in, passing on yer gift to as many people as we need. There's no accounting for punters' tastes. For what they want to see. And then there's freaks fighting too. Which is where the real money is. Because everyone likes a flutter, don't they?'

He began pulling across the right-hand shutter. 'You're a licence to print money, boy. For now anyway. You be a good lad and we'll let you live. We could end up being one big happy family.' Billy paused and ran a thumb up and down the edge of the shutter, and peeled off a splinter of wood. 'If you get half the love I got from my ma, you'll be just fine, boy. She'll be better than yer first one. That one in the paper. You saw how gentle she was with you just now. You love my ma 'n' she'll love you right back.'

'Never,' said James. 'She could never be like my mum.'

Billy bent the splinter in half and flicked it away. 'It's either that or end up being scared shitless of her like most of 'em around here and I know which I prefer. He shrugged. 'My da was a hard bastard. And I know that stepdad of yours is too after what you told us at the farm when Ma was fixing you up. That's why you ran away, en't it?' Billy grinned. 'Mothers and sons are more than just special, en't they?'

The right-hand shutter banged against the black bars and the wagon became darker and darker until there was just a seam of light between the two shutters where they met in the middle. And then the light narrowed further as Billy locked them together.

James tried to shout out that he was still just a boy, that they had made a terrible mistake. But as he formed the words he stuttered, remembering the night on the moor. The grainy moonlight. The dead sheep. He heard the skin splitting on his shoulders and the click of his fingers snapping up out of their joints.

255

James could not be sure what Webster had been.

Or what he himself might become at the next full moon.

It was dark and cool in the wagon after Billy had left. To James it seemed as though he had been buried alive. Or been spun up in a cocoon. He sat thinking about the clues he could remember, trying to fit them together. Webster had been a soldier. He had seen terrible things. His mind had become unhinged. That's what Cook had believed. And that's what James had grown to think too.

But Cook had not been out on the moor.

James reached round and found he still had his pages in the back pocket of his jeans. They were muddy. Torn. The ink had run in places. He smoothed them out and held them up beside the gap in the shutters, studying the bits that weren't smudged, hoping to try and understand something further about what had happened to him. About Webster. About everything that had occurred since the afternoon he'd found the man in the house on the hill.

But he could not find any answers.

When he discovered the newspaper cutting of himself, he stared at his picture for quite some time. And then he stood up and picked up the empty bucket, and placed it by the seam of daylight running between the shutters. He poured water from the wooden cup into the bucket until it was almost full, then waited for his reflection to appear.

He saw a raggedy face. Dark and brooding and dirty. And James muttered and shook his head, and broke the surface of the water. But, when the ripples settled, the face he saw again was not the face of the boy in the newspaper cutting.

He sat looking into the bucket for a long time, questions circling within him, and he could find no way of chasing them away.

Eventually, he stood up and tipped the water through a gap at the bottom of the shutters on to the grass below. Then he rooted around on the floor for a small stone, choosing one with the sharpest edge he could find. He gouged out a vertical line in the wooden wall opposite the bars because one night had passed since Webster had attacked him.

Afterwards, he picked up the pages again, scanning through them until he knew for certain how many more nights it would be until the next full moon.

Twenty-seven.

He would know for sure then what he was. All the doubts about what was true and what was not would be over for good.

He picked up the stone again and began gouging blond-coloured letters into the wood. And, with each one done, the keener his mind became. And when he had finished he stepped back and observed what was written there.

UTRINQUE PARATUS

Taking out the torch from underneath the mattress, he pointed it at the wall, clicking the button on and off repeatedly, lighting up the letters then making them disappear. Every time he saw them, it was a message to himself to be ready, as he repeated over and over that he would try his utmost to escape from the wagon.

It wasn't long before he had started to work out a plan.

39

He had to get stronger first. Once he was out of the wagon, he knew he was going to have to run as fast as he could. But, for now, his body felt like it was made of glass.

He discovered he could walk ten short paces from one end of the wagon to the other before turning round and walking back. Walk. Turn. Walk. Again and again, as long as he could, until his legs and arms became tired and he had to rest. Then he would set off again. Gradually, he started walking with his eyes shut, learning to keep in a straight line, counting every ten steps until it was automatic.

After a while, he found he could be walking anywhere.

Wherever his imagination took him.

He was determined to get there.

And whenever he arrived it was exactly how he wished the place to be. A graceful desert. Or a beautiful beach. Or a hotel with stunning views.

The first time Webster appeared by his side after closing his eyes, James shouted at him to go away, telling him they were no longer friends. But, after he had gone, James was left miserable and empty. So he was glad when his mother appeared soon afterwards.

He told her he was confused, that he wanted Webster far away from him, but close by too. So he asked her to speak to the man and explain how he felt, as well as ask all the questions James needed answering, to help him understand why his friend had done what he had on the moor. There was so much he wanted to know that he was breathless with all the 'whys' and 'hows'.

So they would walk behind James.

Talking.

His mother's soothing voice explaining things, asking questions and, every now and then, the mumble of Webster's deeper, whispered tones. And even though James felt his anger welling up inside, as bright and clear as a bead of water clinging to the lip of the wooden cup Billy had given him, it never broke and he did not shout at Webster to leave again.

James never walked back to the wagon. But, whenever he opened his eyes, he would reappear there, as if by magic, standing in the soft semi-darkness, with light cutting through the cracks in the shutters. Separate from everyone. And everything.

Occasionally, he heard voices in the distance. But he had given up shouting at them because no one ever replied. And no one ever came to see him except for Billy.

Every night the man would appear after sunset, and fold back the shutters and let in the night. He would deliver fresh food and empty the bucket that served as a toilet bowl. Then he would leave James looking out through the metal bars at the sky, watching the stars, if the night was clean and clear, and listening to snippets of sounds from the fairground whenever they caught on the breeze. Electric notes. The whoosh of rides hurling people into the air as they screamed. The bass hum of generators. And, each morning, Billy returned to perform the same duties and then shutter up the cage for the duration of the day.

This was how James lived now.

Perpetually in the dark.

Like an antique in an attic.

But all the time he could feel himself getting stronger.

Walking.

Eating the food brought to him.

Walking again.

Ready for the moment he could escape.

June 19th

40

It was on the fifth night after being attacked on the moor that James decided to break out. He knew this because there were already four vertical lines in the wood. He wasn't going to make it five nights in the wagon.

He sat on his mattress in the dark, waiting for Billy to appear and open the shutters. When he heard the man tramping over the grass, coughing and spitting, James took out the torch and held it in one hand. In the other was one of his socks, the end of it filled out with stuffing from the mattress to make it into a ball, and then lined with the small stones and bits of gravel he had found on the floor of the wagon. Coins from his pockets were in there too. And so were the two batteries from the torch.

James watched the shutters roll back. Billy stared at him.

'All right, boy?'

'Yeah,' he said, one hand clenched around the neck of the sock as he let it dangle out of sight behind his right leg.

As soon as Billy came round to the end of the wagon and thumped up the small set of steps, James ran towards the door. When it opened, he held up the torch, pointing it at Billy's face, and clicked the button. But there was no bright light in Billy's eyes. The man started laughing when he realised, shaking his head, as James clicked the button repeatedly, gasping frantically through clenched teeth.

'You en't catching me out this time.' Billy held out a hand for the torch, as the metal bowl of soup steamed in the other. When James offered it up to him in the flat of his palm, Billy reached forward, leaning down, grinning at the boy until he noticed James's black shoes standing in a corner and peered down at the boy's bare feet.

James swung the sock in his other hand as hard as he could.

The coins and stones and batteries chattered excitedly as they flashed through the air before striking Billy on his cheek, sending him off balance and crashing against the wall.

The metal bowl of soup fell with him to the floor.

James hurdled Billy and jumped off the steps on to the grass. His legs and arms started to pump as he ran barefoot across the field towards a dark border of hedge with a gate silhouetted in the far right corner.

He could hear Billy cursing, and then roaring, as the man righted himself, but James did not look back as he aimed for the gate, the quickest way out of the field. The dewy grass was cold, slick beneath his feet, and he skidded, just managing to keep his balance, as he ran. Excited voices rose from the fairground beyond the caravans away to his left as though cheering him on.

Billy was puffing and shouting behind him, his boots thundering. But James knew he would make the gate in time and began to judge how best to climb it.

But, before he reached it, he saw a pair of headlights sweeping down the lane on the other side of the hedge. A car turned in towards the gate and stopped, shining two full beams of light into the field, making James put up his hands before veering out of their glare. Blinking the light from his eyes, he looked again and saw the driver's door open, and the silhouette of a man stood in front of the car between the headlights, laying his arms over the top of the gate.

James heard a shout for help ready in his throat, but before he could cry out he heard the man laughing and James gasped instead, knowing what it meant.

Another traveller was sitting in the passenger seat, lit up by the interior light of the car, laughing too.

James backed away from the gate, looking along the hedge, trying desperately to find another way out through the dense band of bramble and hawthorn. When he thought he saw a small gap, he ran towards it. But, as he tried to push and then pull himself through, the brambles tore at him. Nettles stung his hands. And soon his jumper was snagged in the hawthorn. The more he struggled, the harder it became to get free.

And then he heard Billy cursing behind him.

A moment later, the man's warm hand closed over James's ankle and yanked him backwards on to the wet, slippery grass.

June 20th.

41

The next morning the old woman visited James again. As Billy prepared the shutters for the oncoming day, the sunlight glinting off the plum-coloured bruise on his cheek, the steel door opened to reveal her standing on the top step wearing a red apron.

She studied the four vertical lines in the wood and the Latin inscription, but said nothing. Her leather pouch had been mended and restrung on a new leather cord, and it clinked against her chest. She smiled at the boy and then took out a small glass jar from her skirt pocket. After twisting off the black plastic lid, she dug out a fingertip of ointment.

'Let me put this on yer shoulders,' she said. 'I've made it for yer wounds, to help them heal.'

James sat quietly as she rubbed it gently into his skin. It was soothing and cool, and the smell reminded him of the ointment that Webster had used to heal the cuts on his face.

Billy stood watching them through the bars with his arms folded.

'I told him if he loves you then you'll love him back.'

'Yes, I will,' replied the old woman and smiled at her son. Then she leant in close to James and whispered, 'You belong to me and Billy now, and that's the end of it. We made a bargain, remember? That farmer and his wife are still alive because of it.'

After she had finished, she slapped her hands together and rubbed them clean on her apron. From its front pocket she drew out a small paring knife, and went over to the wall and scored a horizontal line through the four vertical ones that James had already drawn.

And then she left, locking the door behind her, leaving the boy sitting in the dark, shuttered wagon as she and Billy walked away over the grass.

June 21st

42

The heart was kept in a mason jar, full of salted water and herbs, which sat in the dark of a cupboard in the old woman's caravan. Occasionally, she would take out the jar and hold it up to the light, spinning rainbows in the water. Billy would look away whenever he saw it.

'Put it away, Ma,' he told her finally, after seeing the grey thing once too often, bumping against the inside of the glass, as he sat and drank his tea. 'It en't no thing to be looking at, let alone keep in a jar. Whatchoo holding on to it for anyway?'

But she smiled and shushed him.

'A heart from a man like that is far more useful than gold or money. Least that's what's clear from the stories told before either of us was born or even thought about.'

'So what are you gonna do with it then?'

'Lots of things.'

'Well, I just wish you'd hurry up and get rid of it.'

The old woman stowed the jar in the cupboard and then looked into her son's eyes. 'You freed him,' she said, patting his shoulder. 'You didn't kill him.' Billy stared back at her. He smoothed out the lines on his forehead with the back of a hand.

'Yeah? Well, it's still a burden, "freeing" a man, if that's what you want to call it.' He stood up from the table and opened the door, and let the sunlight warm his face before he left.

After he had gone, the old woman went to the rocking chair and picked up the wooden mannequin from its seat. She inspected the bandage on its broken leg, before sitting it on the worktop beside the stove. And then she took out the jar again. She scrutinized the heart for some time, rotating the jar, observing the mechanism that had pumped life through Webster. She had seen human hearts before, but this one was slightly larger than the others.

'Powerful though,' she whispered to the little man as she held the jar up close to his face, ballooning its painted eyes in the glass. Then the jar went back into the dark of the cupboard because they had many things to pickle and prepare on such a special day.

For it was the summer solstice.

June 22nd

43

It had been seven nights since the full moon and now the eighth was beginning.

In the gloom, James counted the seven marks on the wooden wall again before turning round and sitting back down on his mattress to look out through the bars at the new view in front of him.

Earlier in the day, he had heard shouting in the distance, carried on the wind. When he had rushed to the bars and peered into the thin vertical line of light between the shutters, he had been unable to see anything except for the usual green strip of field. Later, when he heard sounds outside the wagon, he got up from his mattress to look through the gap in the shutters again and saw Billy backing a dirty green Land Rover past the bars.

He wobbled when the wagon jolted suddenly, wondering what was going on. And then he guessed.

When the wagon started moving, he heard the hiss of grass below him and stared out through the shutters at the traveller caravans as they swung into view. Beyond them he could see the fairground being picked apart by people the size of ants and caught sight of the roller-coaster track being winched down in its various parts.

Soon the wheels were picking up speed over a road and James managed to stand up, planting his hands on the shutters to steady himself, and look out through the gap again.

Blue sky.

A hedgerow ticking past.

Trees.

An old white road sign flashed by with the name *Froggington* written in black letters. It meant nothing to James.

At first, whenever a car passed, going the other way, he shouted out, but it soon became obvious no one could hear him. A red sports car did overtake them on a stretch of road. Top down. A middle-aged man wearing a dark suit sitting behind the wheel. But, when James yelled out as the car roared past, the man only looked round momentarily and then focused back on the road.

James could not be sure how long they travelled for.

It seemed like hours, the wagon wobbling and making him sick, his nose and forehead becoming numb against the shutters as his single, staring eye ached.

They stopped once, at a junction, and James saw a young woman pushing a pram along the narrow path beside the road. He yelled as loudly as he could. But, when the woman looked up, she seemed to stare straight at him, without seeing him behind the shutters. He tried wiggling his fingers out through the gap. But, by then, they were already moving again and picking up speed.

When Billy rolled back the shutters as usual for the night, James leapt up to look through the bars to see where they were. Another green field. A knot of caravans and trailers too, parked far away on the other side of the grass beside a hedgerow, the lights in their windows glowing in the dusk. He saw the silhouette of someone walking and then lost sight of them in the failing light. There was no sign of the fair. Not a sound. Just bats clicking circles in the gloom.

'No one'll stick their nose in,' said Billy as he came round in front of the bars. 'Me ma's word's law round here.' He walked away, over the grass, towards the caravans.

James watched the lights in the windows go out one by one. Eventually, the voices dried up long after the bats had vanished. All he could hear was the sound of leaves rustling somewhere out of sight behind the wagon.

He dragged his mattress in front of the bars and sat down, facing the people he knew were sleeping in the little cluster of caravans. As he stared at the new view, he looked for anything that might give him a clue about how to try and escape again.

June 23rd

44

Mist licked the bars and made them sparkle. The field was hidden behind a wet wall of grey, brightening to a hazy orange in one corner as the early morning sun rose.

James shivered. Wrapped the blankets tighter, wondering what had woken him.

Then he heard a sound. Boot steps on the wet grass.

He waited, expecting to see Billy, but it was a much older man who walked straight past the wagon out of the mist, trudging right to left. His blue shirtsleeves were rolled up to his elbows in thick wedges. He was looking down at the wet green shimmer beneath his feet. A white pail of bright red berries was swinging gently by his side.

'Hello?' whispered James, scrambling to his feet. But his voice was papery and soft and full of grit. 'Hello?' he said more loudly. The old man stopped. Turned. Peered back through the mist. He was little more than a blur. James moved up to the wet bars, and stuck out his arm and waved it. 'Over here,' he mumbled. The figure took a few steps forward. A grey, tired-looking man. A ragged scar on the left of his face.

James was sure he recognized him. He tried remembering where or when they had met, but his mind kept slipping. Words started bubbling up in his throat out of his control.

'Help me!' he croaked. 'Please. Help me get out of here.' The man shook his head. 'Please,' said James, his hands tightening around the bars.

'You ain't none of my business,' the man half whispered and then turned round and began disappearing into the mist.

There was mist in James's brain too.

Thoughts broke through it and then vanished again.

He knew there was something important about the man. About the scar on his face.

'Wait! I know who you are. I do. You're a good man. Please. Just let me out.'

But the man laughed and the laughter rang in the droplets of mist.

'You don't know me,' his voice rang back. 'And I don't give a damn who you are, boy.'

James squeezed the grey sludge in his brain. Memories sparkled.

Quickly, he dug out the notes from the pocket of his jeans and ran through the notes in the margins until he saw the name he knew was written there.

'Wait,' shouted the boy.

But the man had vanished.

'You're Gudgeon!'

The squeaking of the pail handle stopped abruptly. A few moments later, the man reappeared for a second time out of the mist. He wiped his forehead with his free arm. Spat into the wet grass. And stared straight at James.

'How do you know my name, boy?'

James heard desperate words inside him. He didn't know what to say at first. There was too much. He wanted to tell Gudgeon about Webster. He wanted to ask him to let him out of the wagon too. But he was cold. His shoulders were sore. His fingers were wrapped around the bars like wire as his mind kept slipping and sliding. When he blinked, he saw the old woman's face. Billy's too.

'How do you know my name, you little bastard?' hissed Gudgeon, edging closer to the wagon.

James shivered. Every time he thought of the right thing to say, the idea wobbled and fell apart. But he knew what he had to do.

He had to make friends with the man.

Talk to him.

Like Webster had done.

Then maybe Gudgeon would let him out too.

'I want to be your friend,' James whispered as he shivered and shuddered. 'You can trust me,' he said and kept nodding as if that was enough. Gudgeon just stood there, the pail hanging by his side, the berries heaped in it shining as brightly as his scar. James hoped that the man would break out into a smile and whisper that he was a friend too. That he would help him. Just as he had helped Webster.

But the man just hawked and spat again.

'Is that right?' said Gudgeon.

James stared into his sneering face. And, suddenly, it was like a key turning in a lock inside him.

'I already know lots of things about you. I can tell you about your wife if you want.'

Gudgeon stood proud, bristling like a thistle, and not giving anything away.

'What about her?'

'I know she died a couple of years ago. She had golden blonde hair and lips as red as holly berries, and she ran away with you when she was sixteen. You gave her a bouquet of daisies on your wedding day,' said James, willing his wandering mind to recall all the details Webster had told him.

The old man stood there, his eyes shining as though he had been slapped in the face. His head tipped slightly to one side as he kept looking at the boy.

'How do you know all that?' he asked. 'Who told you?'

'I know you have three children too,' sobbed James. 'And that none of them stayed with you.'

Gudgeon walked up to the bars and gripped them.

'Tell me how you know!'

James nodded as he steadied himself. He was going to tell the man. But he had to get the words right. He wanted Gudgeon to be friends with him. Everything had to be done carefully. He had to tell him about Webster. But, before he could speak, he heard different footsteps in the wet grass.

Gudgeon stood for a moment, listening too. As though time had stopped.

'You're gonna bloody tell me,' he hissed. 'I wanna know.' And he walked quickly away, disappearing into the mist, clutching the pail to his chest.

James wanted to say something to make him stop, but, when he saw Billy's outline appearing, all the words dried up.

He waited quietly by the bars as Billy walked towards him with a bowl of broth in his hands. The man yawned. Rubbed his face. Then stopped when he saw the trail of footprints printed in the dew in front of the wagon. Billy looked back into the mist and listened. Then he knelt down and inspected the footprints more closely, measuring his boot against one, looking down at it for a long time. When he had finished, he stood up and went up close to the bars.

'Who was here?'

'No one,' said James.

'Someone was. A man.'

'I was asleep. I didn't see anyone.'

Billy grunted. 'You're lying, boy, and liars don't eat.' He poured the broth on to the ground, forming a sloppy pool of steaming brown. Then he pulled on all the bars one by one. When he had finished testing them, he rolled on to his back and disappeared under the wagon. James heard him tapping the floor in places. When Billy reappeared, he walked right around the wagon, banging on the panels of timber with his fist.

James crouched down in a corner when the door opened. But Billy ignored him and looked around the walls, studying them in a few places, before locking the door again. Then he closed the shutters over the bars and left.

45

When Billy banged open the door to Smithy's caravan, he saw him sitting at the folding table, holding a
mug of tea between his hands. Smithy blew away the
steam. Set the mug down. Said nothing. Billy
marched over. Leant on the table. Looked him full in
the face.

Smithy shuddered and looked away as the table
creaked with Billy's weight.

'You been round my wagon again, Smithy?'

Smithy shook his head. 'I en't done owt, Billy.
Honest,' he said. His hands shook. 'I en't been anywhere.
Not at all.' He grinned his mouldy, toothy grin and
shook his head. 'I never done nothing. Nothing.'

Billy slammed down his hands on the table. Glared
at Smithy. And saw nothing in those eyes but fear and
simple-mindedness.

'No,' said Billy quietly. 'But you did though, didn't you? Before?'

Smithy looked down. Looked up. Looked down again. Licked his lips.

'I can't remember,' he said. 'I don't get to hold much of anything in this rotten old head.' And then he brightened. 'I know you taught me a lesson I en't never gonna forget though. Took me thumbs so I'd never forget.'

He held up his hands for Billy to see.

Two healing stumps where the thumbs had been.

He smiled. Shook his head. 'I en't done nothing, Billy.' He reached for the roll-up lying on the table, and managed to scoop it up between both hands and offer it up in an outstretched palm. 'Black Sea Basma,' he said. 'I grew it myself, Billy.'

And Billy ground his jaw, then turned round and left.

For the rest of the day, in the dark of the shuttered wagon, James worked hard on what he was going to tell Gudgeon. He knew the man would come back to see him. To find out how he knew so much.

To begin with, James thought all he would need to do was tell Gudgeon he was Webster's friend. That it would persuade the man to help him. But the more he thought about it, seeing it from Gudgeon's point of view, he realized it might not be enough. To be sure of

Gudgeon's help, James needed to convince him he really had to be freed from the wagon.

But how?

Without a plan, the hollows of his head began to fill with gentle voices whispering to him that he would never be free. They told him he was better off staying in the wagon forever, not having to worry about where he would go if he was out in the world, and what he would have to do to survive there. They reminded him that running away had done him no good at all so far, laughing about what had happened on the moor. And they laughed even harder when he scored an eighth mark on the wooden wall for the night that had just passed. And the voices were slick and wet and cold, and made him shudder.

When they became too loud, James put his hands over his ears, and shouted to try and scare them away. And when that didn't work he stood up and ran his fingers back and forth over the Latin inscription on the wall, telling himself that Gudgeon's appearance out of the mist must have happened for a reason. But the voices chattered and hissed, asking who would ever make such a thing happen in the world.

With the day drawing near to its close, James sat down beside the shutters and leafed through his tattered pages, before the daylight dimmed too much between the cracks, and found what he was looking for. The drawing. The one he had made in the margin beside Gudgeon's name.

It was the face of a man, with a beard and flowing hair, staring up at him out of the page. He remembered drawing it the night he had stayed with Webster in the motel. He tapped the paper thoughtfully, spelling out the three letters of the name he had written down, over and over in his head. And gradually the boy remembered everything Webster had told him in the motel that evening. And, most importantly, he remembered why Gudgeon had helped Webster escape.

As James's mind worked everything through, he began to realize that Gudgeon was no different to him or Webster or Cook, or even the farmer. And none of them were different to anybody else who had ever lost someone they loved or known of somebody who had died.

After the shutters were opened, Billy unlocked the door and walked into the wagon. James took his bowl of broth and began to eat. He could see the knot of caravans glowing in the murk. Someone had lit an open fire. Voices wove in and out of the clatter of pots.

'Well?' asked Billy.

'I told you, I didn't see anyone.'

Billy leant against the bars and watched James eating, and when the boy stopped he told him to go on and finish the bowl because he was waiting to take it back. But James could not finish his meal, nervous about being watched because such a thing never normally happened.

'Suit yerself,' said Billy, plucking the bowl away and slinging the rest of the broth between the bars. 'If you want to eat again, you'll keep yer ears and eyes open tonight, and tell me if you see anyone.'

James nodded.

After Billy had left, he sat down in a corner, and crossed his legs and waited.

And waited.

But Gudgeon did not appear.

Eventually, he lay down on the mattress and looked up at the stars. He watched satellites ticking by. Saw shooting stars rip lines in the dark. And he tried to see if there was anything else he had missed in the night sky despite all the times he had looked.

June 24th

46

When James awoke, he felt something poking him in the ribs.

A stick.

Rattling between the bars.

Gudgeon was holding it.

The early morning light was purple and there was a light drizzle falling, making the air crackle. James rubbed his eyes and sat up.

'That Billy's been waiting up all night,' whispered Gudgeon. 'Hidden in the woods behind you. He's dozing now, mind.'

'He saw your footsteps in the dew.'

Gudgeon leant closer to the bars.

'But you didn't tell him anything about me?'

James shook his head.

'We have to be quiet.' Raindrops rolled down Gudgeon's

nose. They clung to the hairy parts of his face and dripped from the lobes of his ears. 'So you tell me then, how come you know so much about me?'

James nodded slowly, remembering all the time what he had planned to say.

'I know,' he said, 'because I'm an angel.' He stared at the man who stared straight back. The rain grew harder and the grass hissed as it fell.

'An angel?' whispered Gudgeon. His knuckles turned white as he squeezed the bars.

'Billy and his ma cut off my wings so they could keep me,' said James and he pulled down his sweater to show Gudgeon the red scars on his shoulders. The old man hauled in a breath and let it out slowly. He flicked the rain from his face.

'An angel,' said Gudgeon again as though not believing it and yet believing it at the same time. James nodded.

'Your wife's happy where she is now. You don't need to worry about her.'

Gudgeon pushed his head into the gap between two bars until he could go no further.

'I don't?'

'No. She watches over you every day.'

Gudgeon's eyes glistened. Tears rolled down into the wet on his skin, mingling with the raindrops. He choked in his throat.

'Where is she?'

'In a safe place.'

'What's it like?'

'Light and warm. Golden.' Gudgeon kept staring at him, expecting more. But James had no sense of how he should describe the place he was thinking of. And then he remembered where he hoped his mother might be, safe from harm. And where he hoped Cook and Webster were too. 'It's a place where nobody's evil. Where nobody wants anything from anyone else. It's where everybody knows the truth about everything.'

'Is God there too?' asked Gudgeon. He was entranced. Eyes bright and wide, his wet face sparkling.

James juggled words in his mouth, unable to speak, because he was unsure what to say.

But Gudgeon was waiting. Staring. James dug his nails into the palms of his hands and remembered how important it was to tell the man what he wanted to know.

'Yes,' he said. 'God's there.'

Gudgeon smiled. Nodded slowly. He rubbed a forearm over his face.

'Thank you,' he said, and reached between the bars and took one of James's hands, and squeezed it. 'Thank you.'

'I have to get out,' whispered James. 'Please. Help me get me out of this cage.'

301

But Gudgeon let go of the boy's hand and looked down at the ground. 'You belong to Billy and his ma,' he said.

'But they stole me away. They keep me in here where I can't be seen.'

'Where not even God can see you?'

'No.' And James could see Gudgeon wondering whether such a thing could ever be true. 'Billy's ma knows magic,' he said quickly. 'All sorts of things. That's how she's keeping me hidden.'

Gudgeon nodded his head very slowly as he thought it through.

Suddenly, he looked behind him as though he had heard something.

'I reckon he's coming,' he whispered. 'Billy's coming.'

Gudgeon began backing away.

'Wait. Tell me you'll help me.' But Gudgeon kept moving and disappeared from view. 'Wait!'

James heard someone running.

Then a gunshot.

And nothing else.

Billy appeared by the bars. Cursing. Out of breath. His hair slicked back and shining. And James took a few steps back.

'Tell me who it was?' Billy growled.

'I don't know.' James shook his head. 'I've never seen him before.'

'Little bastard!' shouted Billy. He disappeared round the side of the wagon and opened the door, then marched towards the boy who dropped down into a corner. Billy stooped and grabbed him by the throat, making James cry out. 'Tell me it was him,' shouted Billy.

'Who?' cried the boy, tears sparkling on his face.

'Tell me it was Webster.' Billy squeezed harder. 'Tell me it was him. I know it's him. I know he's not dead!'

James blinked. He couldn't breathe.

Billy stared at the boy. Thoughts hammered in his head. He opened his mouth to speak, and then shut it again and let go of James's throat, and the boy gasped for air. Billy marched out of the wagon, slammed the door and locked it, and started pulling the shutters over the bars.

'Don't you speak to nobody, you little wretch,' he hissed. 'Or I'll cut out yer tongue. Do you hear?'

James nodded, watching the world disappear as the shutters were locked into place. But all the time his mind was racing, churning over what Billy had said about Webster.

When he laid the Lanber down on the table in his caravan, Billy stayed still, looking at it, rain dripping off him on to the floor. Then he kicked out at the table leg.

'Bastard gun.'

He towelled down his hair and made himself a cup of tea, and then sat at the table and looked out of the window at the field and the wagon in the distance, with the woods behind it. The fairground was starting to take shape in a field to the left of the trees. He stared at the half-built helter-skelter pointing at the sky, thinking for a while, until his blood had cooled. Taking a slurp of tea, he reached across and picked up a flyer for the fair from the large pile stacked on a chair beside the table. He studied the details silently, and then cursed to himself, and balled up the flyer in his fist and threw it against the wall.

47

Gudgeon sat in his caravan for quite some time, listening carefully for any footsteps or voices outside. But no one came and knocked on his door. Eventually, his hands relaxed. They had been glued tight to the edge of the table in front of him the whole time.

Whenever James's face drifted into his mind, he swatted it back into the dark. But like a fly it kept coming back.

He got up and went to a drawer, and took out an old iron key. He laid it down on the table and looked at it.

'Maybe I kept you for a reason after all,' he said.

After putting the key in his pocket, he checked on the sky and saw patches of blue, and realized the day was set for fine weather. He decided he would take a drive to the coast nearby. He'd smoke. Walk. Think. It would be easy enough to throw the key off the cliff if he felt that was the best thing to do.

'Sod 'em,' whispered Gudgeon when he saw the fair going up beside the woods. And then he glanced at the wagon and thought about the boy behind the shutters.

When he opened the door, he saw Billy, walking straight towards him, carrying a shotgun. Gudgeon gripped the door frame with one hand. The other went into his pocket and closed around the key.

'Hey, Gudge,' shouted Billy, hurrying towards him. 'I'm glad I caught ya.'

'Yeah?' The old man's heart was close to breaking as Billy stopped at the bottom of the steps. 'Why's that?'

'Cos you can fix anything, everyone knows that.' And Billy grinned. 'This Lanber keeps sticking on the upper barrel.' He pointed the gun at Gudgeon and pulled the trigger, and there was no click. Not a sound.

As Gudgeon stared down the black mouth of the upper barrel, a thin trickle of sweat rolled over the bumps of his spine.

'Probably just needs a good clean,' he said. It was as many words as he could muster.

'I done all that,' said Billy, shaking his head. 'It's something else. The workings. You wanna take a look?'

'Could do.'

'You got time now?'

'Yeah.'

'I'll leave it with you then.'

Billy walked up the three steps to the doorway of the caravan, and turned the Lanber around and handed it to Gudgeon stock first. He didn't let go immediately. The two men eyed each other along the length of the gun.

'You all right, Gudge? You look like you seen a ghost.'

'Old age,' said Gudgeon, who tugged the gun free and stood it next to him inside the door of his caravan. 'Some days just ain't as good as others.'

'That right? Long as it en't catching then,' said Billy, smiling.

Gudgeon was sure he could smell the key in his pocket. The rich iron whiff of it. And he was sure he heard it moving and clinking, even though he was breathing as slowly as he could.

'Seriously, if you ever need anything, you know where to go. Me ma an' all.'

'Yeah. Thanks.'

'By the way. My wagon?'

'What about it?'

Billy rolled his fingers back and forth over the door frame.

'There's no way in or out, is there? It's solid, right?'

'Built to last, according to my dear old da.'

'Yeah. That's what he said when me da bought it off him.' Billy looked round the inside of Gudgeon's

307

caravan. Everything in its place. Neat and clean and tidy. Windows full of blue sky and green field. 'I know you're a good man, Gudge. And so was yer da. But I want you to check the wagon over for me anyway. I want you to tell me it's still solid. You got better eyes for it than me.'

'Why?'

'Cos I don't want what's in there getting out. So you give it the once-over, all right?' Billy glanced at the half-built fairground in the distance, checking on its progress, and then he drew out a roll of twenty-pound notes from his shirt pocket and pushed them into Gudgeon's trouser pocket, squashing them down on top of the key that was hidden there. 'Forget the fair today. It'll go up fine without you. I want you to put an extra lock on the door too. That'll cover yer costs and yer time.'

Gudgeon nodded.

'A padlock won't keep Smithy out, if that's what you're worried about. He's got a gift, that boy.' Gudgeon tickled his nose. Coughed and spat on to the grass below. 'I heard he got into your wagon a while back.'

'He did,' said Billy, nodding. 'Poking around where he wasn't supposed to.' He smiled. 'Didn't you hear the rest of it though?'

'Hear what?' When Billy frowned, Gudgeon just shrugged. 'I been away visiting family, ain't I? Only really just got back.'

'Course you 'ave,' said Billy, clicking his fingers. And then he smiled as he did it again, as if he found clicking his fingers amusing. 'Well, I took Smithy's thumbs for it. He won't be going near that wagon again and causing trouble.'

Gudgeon nodded. Wiped the heat from his brow.

'What you got in there then?' he asked. 'The bloody Crown jewels, is it?'

But Billy just smiled back. 'Just you let me know when you're done, Gudge. All right?'

When Billy had gone, Gudgeon closed his door and took out the roll of bank notes and the key from his pocket, and laid them next to each other on the table. He was not sure what he was going to do. Things had become more complicated. As though it was a test set by someone who was watching him to see what happened next.

Setting Webster free had been easy once he had realized how best to go about it. Collecting up Smithy's cigarette butts. Depositing them beneath the wagon steps. Making it look as though it was Smithy who had been talking to Webster and been convinced to pick the lock to set him free. Smithy with half a brain and who was always in trouble on account of it. The story was there for Billy and his ma to read without question.

But now Smithy had no thumbs.

Gudgeon flexed his hands and heard the joints crackle. He tried not to think about what Billy and the old woman might do to him if they caught him freeing what was in their wagon now. He stood there for some time, thinking everything through, until he realized he was staring at the Lanber resting by the door. And he began to wonder why the top barrel had jammed and never fired. Whether it was luck or fate, or something else entirely of another design, a clue perhaps, about what he was really supposed to do. After all, why had he bothered to keep the spare key for the wagon all this time, after finding it in his father's things as a boy? Why had he not thrown it away after helping Webster? And why had he suddenly decided to go and hunt for berries the other morning in the mist only to come across the boy?

He thought about all these things for a long time. Until he decided what he was going to do.

It was late morning by the time he found the problem with the Lanber.

Then he went outside and climbed into his van, and drove over the grass field to Billy's caravan with its bright green lettering.

When he knocked on the door, Billy opened it and yawned before fixing Gudgeon in his sights.

'I've got to go into town to get something for your gun to fix it,' said Gudgeon, glancing at all the paperwork on the table behind Billy.

'Lovely job.'

'And I'll get you a proper padlock there too. I'll fit it on the wagon before it gets dark.'

'Thanks,' said Billy as Gudgeon turned to go. 'You're a star, Gudge. A real good man.' Gudgeon raised his hand without turning round, and got back into his van and drove away out of the field.

In town, after asking around, he found a field sports shop and bought a new mainspring for the top barrel of the Lanber. Then he went to the nearest hardware shop and chose the biggest steel padlock he could find, with a cadmium coating, and bought a stout black hasp. He also had a third key cut for the padlock to match the two in the packet, which he had opened.

It was late afternoon by the time he returned to the traveller camp and saw the big rides of the fair ready and waiting for the evening trade, motionless against the blue sky. He drove across the field right up to the wagon, its shutters still closed, and took out the power drill from among the tools in the back of his van and went about fitting the hasp, putting two self-tapping wood screws into the wooden door frame and two self-tapping metal screws into the steel door. When the hasp was secure, he opened the padlock and pushed the arm of it through the eye of the hasp and snapped it shut. He pulled hard on it to check it was locked.

There was no sound from within the wagon. And Gudgeon said nothing either. After he had finished, he put the power drill back in his van. Then he inspected the wagon, checking the shutters and its underside, as Billy had asked him to do.

'I'm gonna let you out,' said Gudgeon quietly as he walked slowly around the wagon, pressing his hands on the wooden sides. 'I'll do it. But I've gotta come up with a plan so's I don't get caught.' Although there was no reply, Gudgeon knew he must have been heard.

Afterwards, he drove back across the field to his caravan and then worked on the Lanber, replacing the spring for the top barrel with the new one he had bought. When he'd finished, he fired off both barrels to check they were working.

The sun was setting by the time he walked up the steps to Billy's caravan. The fair was already pumping music into the sky. He could just pick out the Orbiter, raising the clusters of cars on its arms, as it started to rotate. Faster and faster it spun, creating a whirring, humming corona of pinks and blues that made his eyes sing and he had to look away.

Billy was not there. So Gudgeon went to his ma's caravan and knocked on the door. When the old woman opened it, he nodded his head.

'All right, Esther?'

'Gudge.'

'I got these two keys for your boy. He'll know what they're for,' he said, holding them up by their tiny metal ring. The old woman nodded, and took the keys and placed them on the counter just inside the door. A black pot was bubbling gently on the stove behind her, blowing out steam whenever the lid lifted off with the heat. He could smell sage and aniseed and lavender. 'I fixed this gun of his too. Needed a new spring. That's why he was having trouble with the upper barrel.' The old woman nodded, and took the gun and stood it inside the door.

'You need paying?'

Gudgeon shook his head.

'All sorted.' When he turned to go, she grabbed his elbow with her bony fingers.

'Money doesn't always do what it should. You look tired. I've got a tonic if you want it. Help you sleep better.'

Gudgeon nodded. 'Thank you.'

He followed her into the dim-lit caravan and waited, looking up at the bunches of herbs dangling from the ceiling, as the old woman rooted through a collection of jars in a cupboard.

When he heard the sound of a rocking chair, he looked up and saw a wooden man sitting on the seat, its undersized legs swinging, one of them bandaged from the knee to the hip. *Swinging like a child's legs,* thought Gudgeon as he felt a chill on his neck and looked away.

'It's in here somewhere,' said the old woman without looking back. Suddenly, the simmering pot on the stove bubbled over and water gushed down over the sides. Quickly, Gudgeon reached across, and lifted the lid and turned down the heat. As the steam cleared, he saw a piece of grey meat bobbing in the water, reflecting the light.

'Supper for your boy, is it?' he asked as she appeared beside him.

'Oh, it's too good for him. It's just my business,' she said and Gudgeon nodded and smiled because he knew not to ask any more. He leant forward over the pot, and breathed in and closed his eyes. He saw a face surrounded with golden blonde hair in the deep dark of himself and smiled.

'My wife used to stuff them with sage and onion. Or put them with other pluck to make haggis.' Gudgeon opened his eyes. 'A sheep's heart for my ram she'd always say when she served it up.' He blushed a little. 'Of course, we were much younger then,' he said, putting back the lid.

The rocking chair suddenly stopped its creaking, but Gudgeon didn't look. He kept his eyes firmly on the old woman as she handed him a small brown bottle of tonic. Then he watched her lift the lid and look down

314

into the pot, and stare at the heart rolling in the water. Her eyes were misty and red. The eyelids almost see-through.

'You all right, Esther?'

She looked over at the gun standing by the door.

'Problem with his gun, you said?'

'That's right,' replied Gudgeon. 'Misfire on the top barrel making it jam.'

The old woman put down the lid on the pot and turned off the heat. She held out a pair of oven gloves to Gudgeon.

'Why don't you take it for yer supper, Gudge?'

'Are you sure?'

'Yes,' she said, nodding her head. 'I don't need it any more.'

48

After scoring a ninth mark in the wooden wall, James sat quietly in the dark, thinking about Webster and Billy, and what had happened on the moor.

He remembered how the single gunshot had echoed up out of the gully and over the gorse and the heather. He recalled seeing the heart in Billy's hand as the man had sat down in the car. There had been an iron smell of blood. The whiff of the shotgun. The bitter stench of boggy mud clinging to Billy's boots. The gleam in the old woman's eye had been as bright as a sunbeam as she'd wrapped Webster's heart in her black shawl.

James turned everything over and over in his mind, and came to the same conclusion every time. Webster was dead. But then Billy's worried face loomed up in front of him and persuaded him to think through everything again. *Why would the man who killed Webster think he was still alive?*

Eventually, James had become tired and dozed, dreaming that Webster had two hearts, but Billy had only taken one of them, allowing Webster to live out his days on the moor because he had felt sorry for the man who was cursed to live as something else.

James had woken later to the sound of a drill. He listened as someone worked on the wagon door, not knowing who, because he could not see anyone through the crack in the shutters. So he sat. Listened. And tried to work out what was happening.

When he heard Gudgeon walking around the wagon, whispering that he was going to let him out, James just nodded. He was too relieved to speak. And he wanted the old man's words to linger all around him in the dark because they were a comfort.

After Gudgeon had left, James drank from the wooden cup until his throat was cool. And for the first time he noticed a warmth inside of him, which he realized was hope.

After Billy had rolled back the shutters to reveal the stars, James heard him walk up the steps and pause at the door. And then the man walked back down and looked up through the bars.

'You're locked up doubly tight now, boy,' he said. 'You want yer food?'

'Yes.'

Billy folded his arms.

'You're sure?' And James nodded. 'I'll go get it then.'

After Billy had disappeared, James listened to the distant noises of the fair. The sounds of faraway voices made his heart shrink and he closed his eyes. And then he thought he heard someone moving in the dark across the grass. He watched carefully and glimpsed the outline of a person beside a section of the hedgerow running around the field. He wondered if it might be Gudgeon. He whispered quietly into the night, hoping that he might hear him on some secret wavelength and come to set him free before Billy returned.

But the old man did not appear.

Gudgeon stood in his caravan, in the lamplight, and laid two keys on the table in front of him. One was the large iron key for the steel door of the wagon, which had been in his possession since he had been a young boy. And one was for the padlock, which had been with him for less than a day.

He rooted around in a drawer until he found an old circular key fob made of brown leather which was sun-cracked and worn. And he slid both keys on to the metal ring of the fob, and put them back down on the table and stared at them again.

'So, Gudge,' he said to himself. 'What's the plan?'

He stood for a long time, thinking about what he was going to do next. It had been risky enough letting out Webster, the man who had been his friend for a while, who had suffered from nightmares as loud and as frightening as his own, which was why they had got round to talking in the first place.

But it would be much more difficult to free the boy. Billy was watching the wagon. Gudgeon sighed and shook his head. The heart the old woman had given him made his whole caravan smell as it sat cooling in the pot on the hob. It made him shudder, and he closed his eyes and stared into the dark until he saw his wife.

'*The boy's an angel,*' she whispered.

Gudgeon nodded his head.

'Yes,' he whispered back.

A sharp knock at the door startled him and his eyes snapped open.

'Gudge?' shouted Billy. 'You there, old man?'

Gudgeon put the key fob in his pocket. When he opened the door, Billy was smiling.

'Looks a good padlock. You got the keys? I need to get in there.'

'Left 'em with your mam. The gun too.'

Billy pursed his lips. Made a thin, wet sucking sound. Nodded.

'Right then.' He turned and walked away.

Gudgeon shut the door and turned round to lean against it.

'It's his ma I should be scared of,' he whispered, looking at the pot. And then he shook his head. 'But if that boy's an angel then there's nothing to be afraid of at all, is there?' He stood there as if waiting for a reply. 'Not if I'm doing the right thing.' He looked up at the ceiling and closed his eyes.

49

His ma's caravan was dark inside. But Billy saw the gun leaning against the wall as soon as he opened the door. Then he saw her outline. She was sitting by the window in her rocking chair. Not a sound.

'Ma?'

He turned on the light, but she did not look up at him. Her eyes flickered beneath their pale, papery lids. Bony shoulders twitched beneath the back shawl. Her lips moved wordlessly as she clutched the leather pouch hanging from her neck. Billy watched her, wondering where she might be. And then a little piece inside of him dropped away for he knew one day she would leave him for good and never come back.

Rubbing away the goosebumps on his forearms, he noticed the two keys on the table, attached to their tiny metal ring, and guessed they were the ones for the padlock that Gudgeon had bought. So he picked them up.

The rocking chair started to tick. His mother looked old and disappointed when she opened her eyes and watched Billy crouch down in front of her.

'Been somewhere nice, Ma?' But all she did was blink as though coming round from a deep sleep. 'Well, I hope so.' He picked up a blanket beside the chair, and tucked it round her knees and smiled. But, before he could stand up, she slapped him hard round the face, leaning forward and grabbing his wrist as he reeled backwards.

'He's here,' she whispered.

'Who is, Ma?' he asked, frightened now.

'Webster. In the woods.'

Billy opened his mouth and then shut it. He looked away and saw the empty mason jar sitting on the work-top beside the stove. The heart was nowhere to be seen.

'You'll bring the boy to me first, and then you'll go and find him. And this time you'll use both barrels whether you need to or not. And you'll show me his body and I'll cut out his heart myself.'

Billy nodded. He looked down at the floor. His lips trembled.

'I'm sorry, Ma.'

She reached up and took his hands in hers, and looked him in the eyes.

'Do it right this time, son.'

'Why's it so important, Ma? For me to kill a man.'

'Because there's a cure to the curse, in the old talk, that's been handed down. A secret.' She paused, as though remembering something she had been told a long time ago. 'If the maker kills themselves out of grief for what they've done, then the one they've cursed will be cured.' She squeezed Billy's hands. 'If Webster ever did that then the boy wouldn't be cursed no more. Then we'd have nothing. Not Webster. And not the boy. And then what would have been the point of it all?'

'And do you believe it, Ma?'

'I can't not. And neither can you. Not if you want the fair to be what you need it to be to prove yer da wrong and so you can get on living yer life, starting a family, and giving me the granddaughter I need so the old ways don't stop with me.' She smiled and looked over at the wooden mannequin which was sitting on the floor against the wall, its bandaged leg stretched out flat beside the other. 'Once he's healed, he'll be just perfect for her like he was for me.'

Billy glanced at the wooden man and then stared at the ends of his boots, thinking about things until they were all just a blur and the tingling in his cheek from her slap had vanished. And then he nodded.

'OK,' he said, 'I'll find him.' And then he stood up, and turned round and left, picking up the Lanber as he went out of the door into the dark.

'I love you,' she shouted after him.

Billy reappeared in the doorway a heartbeat later. Cracked a little smile.

'I know.'

But then his mother shrugged and folded her arms. 'And that's why you lied to me,' she said.

Billy bit the soft inside of his cheek and looked down at the white floor until shapes began to swirl.

50

Gudgeon shut the door of his caravan and walked to the edge of the traveller camp. He drifted out of its glow into the dark and followed the hedge around the field, keeping low, so his outline did not appear to anyone. He stopped when he came to a black tangle of brambles and scanned the open grass. Flat and sheer in the dark. Like the surface of a reservoir. The woods behind the wagon were nothing more than murk, while the lights from the fair splashed across the green canopy from time to time like electric rain. Above the fairground the sky was pearly and bright, like a great arch of marble.

Gudgeon looked up above him. Stars twitched and shimmered.

'You better be watching,' he whispered and then started moving again alongside the hedge. After a few strides, he stopped and crouched low to the ground.

A figure was running over the field towards the wagon. Judging by the shape and the gait, it was Billy. Gudgeon guessed the black stick in one hand was the Lanber.

He looked up at the sky again and nodded.

'Guess I'll wait then.'

Suddenly, Billy stopped in the middle of the field as though listening for something. Gudgeon kept still. Held his breath, afraid it might give him away.

Then Billy ran on and reached the wagon.

Gudgeon did not hear the padlock being opened or the hasp being pulled back. But he saw the steel door opening, glinting in the moonlight.

And, as Billy opened it, someone flashed out from the woods behind the wagon. A man, judging by his size.

The figure was sprinting.

Gudgeon leant forward.

He saw what was going to happen even before it did. As though he had imagined this moment in his sleep and was now watching it for real.

Billy half turned in the open doorway before the moving figure collided with him.

There was a muffled cry. The steel door banged. Both men fell through into the wagon. And then there was nothing except for the sound of Gudgeon's breath behind his ribs.

51

Two men tumbled through the doorway on to the hard, wooden floor of the wagon.

James shrank back.

One of the men was Billy.

And the other was Webster, scrambling to his feet in the grainy dark. Wild black hair in knots. Chest heaving. Clothes ripped and torn beneath his greatcoat. He kicked out at the shape that was Billy, leaving him coughing on the floor.

Picking up the Lanber, he stretched out his other hand to James.

'We need to leave.'

But James did not move, his bare feet stuck to the floor. When he opened his mouth to try and speak, he inhaled the warm dark around him. The corners of his jaw winked, but the words he wanted were hidden down too deep. So he shut his eyes and looked for his mother in the dark inside, hoping she might guide him. And there she was. Smiling. Ready to do what he wanted, to ask Webster all the questions he couldn't about what had happened on the moor.

'Come on,' urged Webster. When James opened his eyes, it was just the two of them again. And Billy. He stepped back when Webster reached out his hand further towards him.

'I won't hurt you,' he said gently. 'I promise.'

But on each dirty fingernail pointing at him, James noticed there was a full moon slowly rising and it made him shudder.

Billy grabbed his ankle, making James gasp. But Webster kicked it away, stamping down on Billy's forearm, and he held out his hand again, waiting for the boy to take it. James looked from Webster to Billy and back again. He heard the fair in the distance, and the wagon seemed to shrink with every heartbeat until he shuddered and blinked, and found himself staring at the marks on the wall. He counted them one by one. All nine of them. And then he read the words he had scratched into the wood.

UTRINQUE PARATUS

Webster saw them too. And when he nodded the boy nodded back.

James steeled himself, trying to forget about the night on the moor and what happened. But he couldn't.

'I can't forgive you,' he whispered. 'I can't, like you couldn't forgive Cook.'

'I know,' whispered Webster, his hand holding steady. 'It's hard. Just like that vicar said.' And, even though James kept nodding, he found himself edging slowly towards Webster, his only friend who had come to rescue him. Who had come back, despite everything that had happened. Who was alive and not dead, as he had thought.

The boy smelt bog and sweat and brambles as he grasped Webster's hand. But this time he didn't falter.

Webster guided him out of the wagon and slammed the steel door behind them. He turned the key that was still in the lock and then flung it away into the darkness. He clicked the padlock shut too. And threw away both keys on the metal ring. He stared at James with fierce blue eyes.

'There's nothing to be afraid of,' he said. 'Nothing.'

And James nodded.

Webster popped out the two cartridges from the Lanber and hurled the empty gun as hard as he could into the dark field.

'Webster!' shouted Billy through the bars of the wagon. 'Webster!'

They turned and ran.

*　　*　　*

The woods swallowed them up. Dark canopies covered the sky and took away the stars. Trunks closed up behind them until they could no longer see the field or the wagon, or any of the lights from the fair. The trees stood silently around them.

Webster stopped when he heard something, and James held his breath and listened to the night.

Somewhere an owl hooted.

A dark shape skimmed between the branches above them.

They watched it wheel round.

'Come on,' said Webster, dragging James, who looked behind him and saw a tawny owl gliding low between the trees. He stumbled as he turned back round and fell to the ground. Leaf litter laughed in his ears. And then claws hooked his hair. A beak hammered on his skull. James gasped. He screamed.

Webster flung out his arms at the owl, and the creature tried to take off with its claws still caught in the boy's black jumper. James screamed again, and Webster tore off the jumper and flung it away with the bird still attached. He threw his arm around the boy and they stumbled on.

When he looked back, the owl was gone. But the bitter smell of the old woman was all around them as they gulped in the fresh night air.

52

Billy stood at the bars, swaying with rage. Gudgeon looked up at him.

'I thought I heard some—'

'The bloody keys, Gudge,' shouted Billy, pointing out into the dark field. 'Find the bloody keys.'

Gudgeon unhooked his hands from the bars, and walked away and stood staring at the ground. But he was not looking for the keys. He was searching for something to make sense of what had happened.

He had not recognized the man who had attacked Billy and rescued the boy. It had been too dark to see anything clearly.

But he knew who it was just the same. Because he had heard Billy shout out the man's name. Twice.

It was Webster. Webster came back.

'Gudge, over there,' screamed Billy. 'Look over there!'

Webster's back. He rescued the boy.

Gudgeon's brain ticked.

They know each other then.

So they must have talked to each other before now.

Told each other things.

Just like I talked to Webster.

And told Webster things too.

'Gudge, can you see them? Can you see the keys?'

Gudgeon's scar was on fire.

The boy knows the things that Webster knows.

So maybe the boy's no angel after all.

'Gudgeon!' screamed Billy again.

But the old man barely heard him.

Maybe the boy's no angel after all.

The leaves on the trees laughed as a gentle breeze caught them. The grass under his feet prickled. Stars winked down, and the cold space between him and the sky yawned wider. Gudgeon panicked suddenly and put out his hands to steady himself. He took a deep breath.

'Gudgeon!'

I got to know for sure.

He turned and marched back to the wagon, fingers searching in his pockets for the leather key fob, and fitted the smaller key into the padlock and turned it. The large iron key crept into the steel lock and the door opened. But, before he could ask Billy anything, a tawny owl skimmed past him, hooting, making him turn and duck. He stared into its eyes as it passed, recognising them immediately, for the last time he had looked into them they had been staring at him in the old woman's caravan.

Billy patted him on the arm as he ran down the steps.

'Good man, Gudge,' he said as he sprinted towards the woods, following the owl as it hooted again, before disappearing into the canopy.

'I'll come with you!' Gudgeon cried out.

'Come on then,' roared Billy as he made for a gap in the trees.

And Gudgeon followed him because he wanted to know the truth.

Just as he had always done.

53

Webster and James stumbled between the trees, Webster pulling the boy until his arm ached and his legs burned. He turned round to yell at James to work harder at keeping up, but the barefooted child was thin and dirty and wretched. Tears had cut bright paths through the grime on his face.

Webster stopped. Dug down into a pocket of his greatcoat. Found the battered plastic bottle of water that was always with him and offered it to James after unscrewing the top. The boy looked at the bottle and said nothing for a moment, and then took it and drank deeply, and wiped his mouth.

'Where are we going?' James asked, shuddering as the water trickled through him.

'Away.'

'Away where?'

Webster took the bottle back, and screwed the top back on and dropped it into his pocket.

James was still looking at him.

'I don't know,' he said, shaking his head.

'I thought you were dead,' whispered James.

'Maybe I should be.' Webster could not stop staring at the scars on James's back. 'Did I do all of that to you?' he asked quietly. When the boy said nothing, Webster looked away. 'All I remember is your voice. Calling me across the moor.' His shoulders bunched, then dropped and shivered. He began to sob. 'It wasn't me. It wasn't.'

James wanted to shout. To scream. But he didn't. All the anger inside him had gone. And so had his fear. He took a deep breath.

'I know,' he said, and slid his hand into Webster's and squeezed it.

Webster wiped his eyes. Stared at the ground. Shuffled through the leaf litter with a black boot as if looking for something beneath the mulch. James noticed he was wearing an old trainer on his other foot without any laces.

'We're the same now, you and me,' whispered Webster. 'And there's no cure for it. That's what the old woman said. There's no way out of this life we have now.'

'But . . . it isn't . . .' And suddenly James took a step back, shaking his head as his stomach prickled, for he could feel a panic growing there. 'I don't feel any different. Are you sure? Is it really true?'

Webster nodded. 'You'll know what I know at the next full moon.'

James kept staring up at him, trying to think up questions to ask, but all that came to him was the memory of how life had been after his mother had died. That none of it had felt true, but he had come to accept it was, even though he could not make any sense of it all.

They heard footsteps nearby.

Webster crouched down, pulling James close to him, as a figure emerged in their eyeline, drifting between the tree trunks. The black shape of a man.

'Who is it?' whispered James as he began to shiver. Webster said nothing, watching as another figure appeared. When he noticed a tree trunk lying close by, he pulled the boy after him and they lay down on the ground, tight behind the log. They listened as the two figures came closer. And then the footsteps stopped.

'You see 'em, Gudge?' said a voice.

'No.'

It was quiet for a while and James wanted to look up, but Webster held on tight when he felt him trying to move.

'They're here somewhere,' came Billy's voice again. 'We'll find 'em.'

'What are you going to do with them?'

'The boy goes back to the wagon. The other one . . .' Billy's voice trailed off. He hawked and spat. 'Well, me ma wants him dead.'

'Why's that?'

'Because it's important.'

'But why?'

'Because she says so. And that's all you need to know, Gudge.'

'Is it cos he's not cursed no more?'

'How do you mean?' Billy's voice sounded surprised. 'What you say that for? What's all that to you?'

'And the boy?' gasped Gudgeon. 'What about the boy?'

All James and Webster could hear was a boot drifting back and forth through the leaves.

'You're the one who let him out,' growled Billy's voice. 'En't you? You're the bastard who let Webster go. It weren't nothing to do with Smithy at all. Whatchoo let him out for, you dopey old sod?'

Suddenly, there was a scuffle in the leaves. Heavy breathing. A whimper. The sound of someone in pain.

'Whatchoo let him out for?' shouted Billy again.

'To help him!'

'Help him? You stupi—'

'*Aggh!* No! Stop! I'll help you get 'em back,' shouted Gudgeon. 'I will. But just tell me about the boy. What is he? What is he really?'

'He's cursed too! Just like Webster. What do you think?'

The two men were breathing hard as they struggled. And then someone thumped heavily to the ground with a grunt and rolled in the leaf litter.

Webster felt the boy's heart hammering in his own chest as they lay wrapped in each other's arms.

The sound of a boot kicking something soft. And then again.

'*Aggh!* OK,' shouted Gudgeon eventually. 'OK!' he yelped. 'You're right. I ain't nothing but a dopey old sod.'

'You got that right,' shouted Billy.

'I'll kill Webster meself. I'll put things right between us on account of what I done.'

'Yeah,' said Billy, laughing. 'Yeah, you bloody will. And killing Webster'll just be the start of it.'

The two men were breathing heavily. And eventually a set of footsteps started up as one of them walked off. And then the other man stood up, brushed himself down, and started walking too. And both sets of footsteps faded away in the dark.

When he was sure the men had gone, Webster peered up over the log. Nothing but trees. But then he saw the owl flying low, quiet as snow. It skimmed over them, and then circled back and began to hoot.

Webster was already up, dragging James after him.

Shouts flashed behind them.

338

Footsteps cannoned up off springy turf.

James thought he saw ghostly figures moving ahead of them in the dark between the trees. He rubbed the sweat from his eyes and looked again. His mother was there, holding out her hands to him. Cook was waving and smiling. Gudgeon's wife was sitting on a branch, together with the farmer's grandson, and they were calling down. James cried out and looked away. Tried to turn round. Webster gripped the boy's hand tighter, dragging him on. But James pulled back harder. Slowing him. Weighing on his arm.

'They're going to kill you,' sobbed James. 'You'll be dead like everyone else. You'll be dead like Cook. And Mum. And Gudgeon's wife. And the farmer's grandson. You'll be gone like them. And I'll be all alone.'

Twigs crackled close behind them. Webster did not look back as he pulled James on.

'Do you want to go back to the wagon?' he shouted. 'Is that what you want?' His voice raged. 'Is that what you want?' screamed Webster.

The shock of it started James running again.

Between the trees they saw a glowing orange dome in the sky. They heard distant laughter. Generators churning.

A pink balloon drifted up through the light, its string trailing, and disappeared into the dark.

They kept on running, towards the fair.

54

The hubbub swallowed them up. The smell of bark and leaves and damp faded. Now it was burnt sugar. Hotdogs. Salt and vinegar.

They stopped in a dark spot, hidden beside a white canvas stall with cheap prizes balanced on blocks of wood. Hoops clattered as they landed. Somewhere in the distance a cheer went off like a firework.

They stood beside the stall for a long time, checking the dark behind them. Looking into the dribs and drabs of people moving up and down the grassy avenue under the lights in front of the stalls.

Webster wanted to drift in among the thin crowd and try to disappear. But James worried that people would stop and stare at him because of the wretched state he was in. Or that someone would recognize him from his picture in the newspapers and alert one of the policemen they had seen wandering up and down, radios pinned to their chests. James told Webster they would never be allowed to see each other again if he was spotted.

'I don't have anyone else,' whispered James, grabbing Webster's hand and squeezing it.

'Neither do I,' replied Webster.

So the two of them moved on, picking their way round guy ropes and the backs of tents and generators, looking for a clue as to what they should do next. When they found an old white van, Webster peered into the cab, but there was no key in the ignition.

He crept round the back of the vehicle. The two rear doors were unlocked. Three Winchester rifles with silver barrels and black wooden stocks lay on a sheepskin rug. Two white styrofoam cups beside them on their sides, half-moons of tea in the bottom of both.

Webster closed the doors as the boy grabbed his arm and pulled him gently round to the side of the stall they were behind. James pointed into the thin lines of people walking up and down the grassy avenue in front of them. The old woman was standing in the middle of everyone, her black shawl wrapped about her shoulders, one hand toying with the leather pouch strung around her neck.

No one seemed to notice her and Webster wondered if he might be seeing just her spirit. But, when Billy appeared beside her and started speaking, that idea died inside him. She was there in her flesh and bones and skin.

Billy soon vanished again, but the old woman waited where she was, the world going on all about her.

Webster heard the popping of gunshots nearby. He followed the sounds until he was looking at a father, and perhaps his son, standing side by side in front of one of the stalls, a shooting gallery. They were each firing a Winchester rifle with a silver barrel and a black stock at metal ducks, and pinging them down with pellets.

'Watch where she goes,' said Webster, and James nodded and kept his eyes on the old woman.

Webster returned to the white van. Opened the doors again. Took out one of the Winchester rifles. Nothing in the chamber or the cartridge. But he slid the gun beneath his coat anyway and went back to the boy.

James pointed and Webster saw the old woman disappearing behind a stall where a steel wheel was churning pink candyfloss.

'What are you going to do?'

But Webster said nothing. He kept low, skulking past the backs of the stalls. And all James could do was follow him. His mind was worn through. The broth he had been eating for however many days nipped at the back of his throat.

Webster stalked the old woman, flitting behind the stalls as she moved down the grassy avenue among the punters. When she stopped to look round, Webster crouched down and pulled the boy towards him.

'I need you to walk out and let her see you.'

'Why?' said James, looking at the rifle. 'What are you going to do?'

'I need you to distract her. Lead her back here behind the stalls.'

'We should just go.'

'I won't let anything happen to you. I promise.'

'We should leave.'

'If we do, they'll keep on looking for us.'

James thought it through. He knew what Webster meant.

As he started walking out from behind the stall, Webster pulled him back, looking down into James's eyes.

'There's nothing to be scared of. I'll be watching all the time.'

James nodded.

Thoughts flashed.

He stumbled out a little past the stall.

And then, a moment later, he turned away from the avenue and headed back into the dark. There was an old black car parked behind the next stall along and, as James passed by, he looked in the wing mirror and saw the old woman's reflection.

She was following him.

Something dark licked up his shins. He wobbled. His breathing was thin inside him. The old woman's voice slipped into his head and told him to turn round. And he had no choice but to do as she asked.

She kept whispering as he turned to look at her, the leather pouch twisting through her fingers. James took one step. Then another. He shivered as she licked her lips.

Webster drew up silently behind her and swung the rifle like an axe at the back of her knees. There was a thud. The sound of something cracking. The old woman cried out as she fell.

James felt the dark slip back down his shins and into the ground. His legs became his own again. He stood watching as Webster rolled the woman face up and ripped the leather pouch from her neck. He planted his single black boot on her chest as she tried to stand up.

'Anything but the answers and I'll burn this leather pouch of yours and everything in it. Understand?'

She lay still and then nodded.

'Tell me how to cure this curse.'

'There is no cure,' she said. 'I've told you. There's no way to lift the curse.'

'There has to be.'

Webster leant down on the gun, pressing the butt of the stock against the old woman's knees.

'If there is then I don't know one,' she gasped.

'You're lying. Why do you want Billy to kill me? Why's that so important? Is that something to do with a cure? Is that so you'd keep the boy cursed forever?'

The old woman groaned. Her black shawl had fallen from her shoulders and she seemed to be sinking into a gaping hole in the grass.

'Tell me,' shouted Webster and he raised the gun above her head as he stood harder on her chest.

'Yoo'se got it right,' said a voice. Billy emerged from the dark with his arms up, palms showing. 'There is a cure.'

The old woman swore a string of bitter words.

'What else am I gonna do, Ma?' said Billy. 'He's holding the gun or en't you noticed?'

But the old woman shouted out. Shook her head.

Webster jammed the gun down on the ground beside her head and she whimpered. He raised the gun again above her white rickety neck and stared at Billy.

'So tell me the truth, Billy. If you want to save your ma.'

'The maker has to kill himself and that way he'll lift the curse from the one he's attacked,' Billy said.

Webster heard the fair. He heard his heart. He heard the old woman gasping. All in a heartbeat. And then he was shouting. 'Where's the other one? Where's Gudgeon?'

'He went round the other way. If you and the boy want to go then go. Good luck to you. You're more trouble than you're worth. I give you my word I won't be coming after you.'

The old woman was shuddering, trying to move from under Webster's boot.

'Ma! It's over. Just lay still.' Billy took a few steps forward and Webster raised the gun higher above her, ready to bring it down. Billy stopped. And then he turned his back on Webster and stared directly at James, and held out his arms on either side of him, his palms upturned.

'I'll let the boy go. You can watch me. Then you can go too. Just like on the moor. Just leave my ma alone, you hear?' Billy stood immobile. All James could see were his teeth. Like a crescent of moon. 'Mothers and sons are special, en't they?' he shouted at the boy.

'Go!' yelled Webster. 'Go on, James.'

James turned and ran.

And he kept going.

And going.

Until he heard someone cry out behind him.

He looked back.

Webster was lying face down on the grass with Gudgeon standing over him.

The old man kicked him hard, and picked up the gun and glued the end of the barrel to Webster's back,

346

nailing him to the ground. The old woman was already on her hands and knees. She was scrabbling at one of Webster's hands, biting at it. And then she rose unsteadily to her feet, one leg bent at an ugly angle, the leather pouch dangling by its cord from her hand.

James blinked and it seemed to last a thousand years.

And then Billy was sprinting towards him.

'Run!' shouted Webster as loudly as he could.

The boy turned.

His legs moved.

His arms pumped.

But everything was weak and bloodless, and heavier than stone. He looked ahead, into the dark of the field stretched out in front of him, and he knew that he would be chased down. He was tired of running into the dark and not knowing what he would find there. So he veered left. He looped back round the tents and stalls towards the fair, and the lights and the people milling up and down the avenues.

And he knew that he was running back to Timpston.

Yet there was nothing he could do about it.

There was nowhere left to go.

James heard the old woman's voice inside him. Each of her words was a lead weight dragging him down. The lights of the fair played over him and he reached out his arms as though trying to pull himself towards them.

But the old woman was whispering to him.

And Billy was breathing hot behind.

Webster saw the boy slowing down. And he could hear the old woman muttering.

He kicked out at Gudgeon who flinched and tottered back, allowing him to roll over on to his back. Webster caught a glimpse of the stars and then Gudgeon was standing over him again, grinning, before pushing the mouth of the gun hard into the socket of his right eye.

Webster grabbed the barrel with both hands to push it away and he heard a dry click as the trigger was pulled.

Nothing but the sound of Gudgeon swearing as Webster tore the gun free and swung it hard at Gudgeon's knees, cutting him down.

Webster was up before the old woman knew what was happening.

As soon as he pushed her to the ground, her muttering stopped. And then he reached down and ripped the leather pouch from her hand.

And, when he looked up, he saw James running on again.

And then the boy vanished beyond the line of tents.

When James reached the grassy avenue of people, nobody noticed him at first.

He screamed.

People stopped and looked.

Ice creams melted over fingers.

Mouths ground to a halt.

Someone pointed at the half-naked boy in front of them.

James fell to his knees and began to sob as a small crowd gathered. Through the ring of shins around him he could see Billy at the edge of the avenue, standing by a white canvas tent. But, at the sight of all the people, the man backed away and disappeared into the dark.

Someone pushed through the people, and crouched down beside James and held his hands.

It was Webster. He was whispering. Instructions tumbled out of him. James barely understood them. He was shaking. Then nodding his head. When he tried to speak, Webster shushed him.

'Don't be scared,' he said so quietly that only James could hear.

Someone wrapped a coat round James's bony shoulders. Voices rippled. Shouts rang. Cameras clicked.

When he looked up, Webster was gone. James looked around for him, but the man was gone.

55

The slap of his palms on the cold metal rungs made the whole structure ring. It was a long way to the top of the scaffolding and the rack of spotlights bolted there.

Despite the climb, his mind was perfectly calm. The simple plan mapped out inside him made sense. Everything seemed so clear, so perfectly resolved, as if it had been intended all along. His breath barely moved as he reached hand over hand, and climbed steadily higher, thinking about the boy, imagining the life ahead of him.

When he reached the top, he hooked his feet into the latticework of scaffolding to hold himself steady. And then he drew out the old woman's leather pouch from his greatcoat pocket and ripped it open, scattering the seeds and pebbles and tiny bones. He listened to their musical sounds as they bounced off the scaffolding and when it was quiet again he threw away the pouch, watching it through the air until he lost sight of it.

The bright lights were burning the top of his head and his cheeks and his lips, and he raised a hand to shield his eyes. All around him was the dark, trying to touch him, but the lights kept it back as they hummed and shone. Down below him, Webster could see a small crowd of people.

He tried to look for James, but it was impossible to pick him out. But he knew the boy would be all right. He had made James promise to be braver than he could ever hope to be, reminding him over and over what the vicar had told them in the church. And then Webster had apologized. For not being as brave as James had wanted him to be.

He drew out the battered old bottle of water from his greatcoat pocket and unscrewed the top. He drank until it was empty and the plastic sides bowed, and then he screwed the top back on and hurled it into the dark.

Then he closed his eyes.

He imagined the heat on his face was the sun in a foreign, war-torn land. And in the dark inside him he saw that little girl hanging by her neck from the branch of the tree. He kept staring, and slowly the dark began to warp and became something else. It was the wall in the bedroom of the old house where he had first met James, which the boy had painted black, and on which he'd chalked up all his ambitions for the future. And the heat on Webster's face became the sun shining in through the big bay windows as he remembered sitting on the sofa in that bedroom, staring at the wall and smiling.

And under the lights Webster felt himself smiling again, for he had never been so grateful to know a person and see their hopes and dreams.

As he pushed himself off, he was weightless. The wind took away his breath.

He opened his eyes, flung back his head and stared up into the lights above him, the dark beyond them growing smaller and smaller as he fell.

When his greatcoat flapped and flew up around his ears, he lost sight of the dark forever.

July 3rd

56

James stood in the kitchen. His stepfather was sitting at the table, staring at him. In front of him lay a newspaper with a picture of James on the front page and a headline:

Missing Boy Saved

It was the first time they had been alone in the house since James had been found at the fair. There had been police and doctors in the hospital, and then reporters and social workers when James had finally returned home. And they had all done their jobs. And now here they were.

The two of them.

James and his stepfather.

Together again.

In Timpston.

'You didn't say anything to anyone?' asked his stepfather.

'No.'

'Why not?'

'I didn't want to. I thoug—'

'What?'

'That things might be different now.'

A tiny muscle flickered in the corner of the man's mouth and James wondered if his stepfather was trying to tell him something had changed, but couldn't find the words. But, before he could say anything to try and help, the man gave up staring at him and grunted, and turned the newspaper over and looked out of the window.

Neither of them spoke for a long time, but James was expecting something to happen at any moment. There were heartbeats in his wrists. His skin was paper-thin. So when his stepfather stood up suddenly, scraping back the chair, and walked towards him, James was ready. But, instead of cowering or moving away, he stood tall, looking straight up into his stepfather's eyes, just as Webster had told him to do.

'I forgive you,' he said quietly.

'You've got that the wrong way round,' growled the man and slapped the table top beside him.

James wobbled. He swallowed down the ringing in his ears. And he kept standing tall, remembering the instructions Webster had whispered before leaving him surrounded by the people at the fair, with their murmurs and their gasps, as they had crowded him like cattle. He heard those last three words again.

Don't be scared.

'I forgive you for everything you've done.'

His stepfather's head jerked to the right as if he had been slapped across the jaw.

'What did you say?'

'For everything you've done and what you're doing now.'

The man curled his fingers into a fist and raised it.

Don't be scared.

'I forgive you for what happened to Mum,' said James, choking on his tears. 'I forgive you. I do. And I'm sorry too, for everything I've ever said.'

His stepfather's fist trembled as if some great force was attempting to break it apart. Looking down at the boy, he tried to say something, but the words caught in his chest and all he set loose was a whimper.

James's eyes seemed to swallow him whole.

Don't be scared.

'I forgive you,' whispered James again. And each word was made of steel. And his stepfather shrank beneath their weight as though unable to bear them, his knees buckling, his shoulders hunching, and his arms tucking in and folding across his chest.

He whispered something and James bent closer to hear. And, when the man repeated it and reached out and held his hand, James nodded gently and whispered something back.

He stood awkwardly over the sobbing man, recalling what the vicar had told him and Webster in the church that day.

The best and the simplest way to defeat dark and evil things is through love.

And he glanced up, out of the window, remembering the first time he had met Webster, and saw the house still there, sitting like a boulder on the hill.

And then he had to look away.

James walked up the hill towards the house. It was nothing more than a grey stone lump of a building with a rotten roof, and crumbling walls, and ceilings fogged with cobwebs. But he wanted to be alone there, with his dreams and ideas, which he knew were chalked up on the black painted wall in the biggest of the bedrooms.

As he began remembering everything he had ever written there, he drew out the newspaper cutting, which no one had been allowed to take from him, and his hand shook as he stared at the picture of himself. And then he tore the cutting into strips and threw them away into the wind. He wondered if anyone else might be watching. And he smiled in case they were and they were smiling too.

When he reached the rotten back door, which had once been white and full of glass, he dragged it open and ran straight through the kitchen, then up the wooden staircase, and arrived breathless on the landing. He waited as he caught his breath, remembering the first time he had seen Webster sitting on the old sofa, looking at the wall, and then he tried hard to think of all the good things that had happened after that.

His heart prickled as he walked into the bedroom and saw the empty seat and the dent in the cushions, so he looked away, staring up at the writing on the wall.

Something caught his eye immediately, written in a different hand in the bottom left-hand corner.

Your mum'll be proud of you whatever you do . . .
. . . and so will I.

James read it over and over until he heard Webster speaking the words, as if the man was close by in a place the boy couldn't see. And then he took a tissue from his pocket and ran it up and down the wall, erasing everything he had ever written there, leaving only the words that Webster had written.

Chalk dust swirled. It made him cough and his eyes itch. And he walked to the big bay windows, and prised one open and breathed in the warm, clean air.

As he looked out, he noticed for the very first time that the trees, which had grown up in the fields and the hedges in the distance, had done so without the hand of man. And, as he looked down on to the grass verges on either side of the lane, looping down around the hill, he knew the plants there would die and then grow up again according to a story far older than anything imagined and written down in books.

Turning back to look at the wall, he stopped when he noticed a single flower growing by his foot, snaking up out of a spot where the floorboards met the wall. He knelt down in front of it, wondering how long ago the seed must have snagged and taken root.

The red oval petals were arranged perfectly in a ring, each one overlapping the other, radiating from a pimpled yellow centre crusted with pollen.

Its fine white hairs prickled his fingers as he grasped the slim green stem.

Staring into the delicate face of the flower, his hand began to shake as he sensed a whole host of mysteries contained there that he could never hope to understand. Letting go, he closed his eyes and was amazed at what he discovered as he stared into the dark inside him. For it was full of the same mysteries too.

And James could not remember a time when he had ever noticed such a thing before.

Acknowledgments

Writing this book has taught me that an author does not create a novel alone and I would like to thank everybody who has helped me along the way.

In particular I would like to thank Clare George for all her guidance as well as Ahmad Abu-el-ata, Marilyn Denbigh, Bella Honess Roe, Joe Marriott, Felicity Notley, Stephanie Smith, Shelley Instone, Emma Timpany and Olly Wicken who provided me with their valuable thoughts and comments.

This book would not have been possible without Madeleine Milburn, who works so hard, believing in the words I write and encouraging others to believe in them too.

I am indebted to my editor, Jane Griffiths, for all her patience and input and to all at Simon & Schuster, especially Ingrid Selberg, Kat McKenna, Laura Hough, Elisa Offord and to Paul Coomey for all his hard work creating the cover.

In addition I must say thank you to all those who have supported me during the writing of this book - The Queen Street Writers, Telltales, Dave Couch, Angus and Hester Macdonald, Nick Roe, Priscilla Short and Matt Wheeler.

Thank you too to my Aunt and Uncle and of course to my Mum and my two sisters whose love has been so important.

Read on for an exclusive prequel story . . .

Ransby and the Robin

April

School was nothing. It was not real life. Most kids never bothered themselves about it. They talked instead about what they would do after class each day. In the holidays. After they had left the school entirely because they had their whole lives ahead of them. No one ever talked about school.

But for James school was lots of things. It was writing and learning and escaping to different worlds. And as long as there was no mention of home or his stepfather he was happy.

As far as most of the other kids were concerned, James was different. And being different hurt sometimes. But everyone else stopped bothering him after Ransby arrived one freezing morning in April.

He appeared steaming snort and mist, leaving big black prints in the frost, as he pushed past the other kids streaming through the gates on the first day of the summer term.

When he sat down in James's class and looked around, everyone else's eyes shone electric greens and blues and browns. It was like being trapped with a tiger.

Ransby was far bigger than everyone else, with acne composting on his face and a crew cut showing off the corners of a big, square head. His white shirt looked too small, the cuffs peeled back across forearms made of heft and black hair, and his neck had seeped over his tie and collar into three doughy rolls. The boy was so large his knees wouldn't fit under the desk so he sat with his legs outstretched, the joints in the chair-back popping whenever he moved.

Over the course of that first day rumours grew about Ransby and where he had come from and what he had done. Most of the class thought they were true except for two boys sitting at the back, whispering and giggling whenever he turned around and glared. Before the end of the day they were found sitting in a stairwell together, licking blood from their lips, their noses wriggly as tail fins between their thumbs and forefingers.

They swore it was an accident.

But nothing like that had ever happened before.

'My nan said you don't kill the goose that lays the golden eggs,' Ransby growled to the others later that week, when the teacher was late, and James was scribbling out answers to his maths homework for him.

Everyone knew what he meant. They'd all noticed his hands by then, which were bigger than most of the teachers'.

So no one bothered James after Ransby arrived. If they did it was only to ask for help with their homework too, joking how they wished they'd thought of asking him before.

Occasionally, James would catch sight of Ransby walking through the town after school, like glimpsing an ogre escaped from a fairytale, lumbering through the streets in search of a way back to its own peculiar world. Sometimes Ransby was smoking. Sometimes he was swigging from a can of beer. Or both.

People stepped off the pavement when they saw him

coming. Some even stepped around his shadow, which was the only company Ransby ever kept. When James started to notice how often the boy glanced back at the people who'd passed him by he decided he knew how a secret part of Ransby felt. So he decided to follow him.

Somehow it seemed to matter.

As if they could keep each other company in some manner that suited them both.

It was a warm afternoon, with the trees showing just a shimmer of green in their tips, when James followed Ransby properly for the first time after school. They stopped eventually, James peering round a corner made of red brick as Ransby stood beside a group of schoolboys crowded round in a meaty, jeering ring.

Looking through the wobbly arches of daylight between their legs, James caught glimpses of a fledgling, a tiny brown robin, fluttering up then jerking back down like a toy on a piece of string.

Whenever the bird flapped too close to any of the boys they rose up on the balls of their feet, like Elvis, their shoulders melting as both arms started waving, their cupped hands scooping up the air around them.

Ransby swigged his bottle of beer as a foot tried stamping the robin flat...

... and missed ...

... and the sole of the shoe slapped the pavement hard, sending its owner tottering into the wall.

Everyone laughed except for Ransby who drained his beer to suds then bashed his way through the ring of bodies, brandishing the empty bottle like a glass dagger, before kneeling down and grabbing the tiny bird in a large white fist.

He held it up to his ear and smiled and nodded as if on the phone, and then walked away ignoring the shouts and swearing that caromed round the street, as if the houses themselves were joining in.

364

Yet none of the boys dared follow him.

But James did, drifting like a ghost past cars and street corners, because he wanted to know what was going to happen to the tiny bird. It mattered to him, although he couldn't find any words to explain quite *why*. All he kept imagining was just how scared the robin had to be in the sweaty dark of Ransby's hand.

It was hot and the sun squeezed him like a sponge, soaking his white school shirt, turning it into a film under his blazer. He felt like a hunter stalking a great beast without a gun. And he tried not to think about what might happen if Ransby saw him, afraid of it coming true if he imagined it for too long despite telling himself the world did not work in such a way. But anything seemed possible with Ransby ahead of him in the distance, lurching like a troll, his backpack like some boil or cyst bubbled up between his giant shoulders, his huge fist held aloft.

He followed Ransby all the way through Falconbury into a pretty street with large houses on either side set back from the road, with gravel drives that moved if he stared at them for too long. And he watched Ransby let himself into a house with a white front door, a semi-circle of glass fanned above it.

James leant against a wall and waited, crouching down when his legs began to ache. Eventually, he left because he knew his stepfather would be angry if he was back too late.

Because that was how his life was.

James wanted to ask about the bird, to reassure himself it was safe. But it was difficult to ask Ransby anything without admitting he had followed him, even after doing his maths homework for him the next morning and handing it back before the lesson started. So James trailed him at lunchtime to see if he could find out more about what might have happened to the robin.

Ransby only went as far as the local burger bar where he bought a bag of chips and ate them one by one, studying a drunk man who was causing trouble at the counter by shaking out drops of vinegar onto the floor and frosting it with salt. When Ransby rolled his chip paper into a ball and asked him to leave, the man just laughed and yanked the boy's tie and squeezed his cheeks, then turned round and ordered a burger as he swigged from a bottle of vodka. So Ransby grabbed a handful of the man's ginger curls and dragged him out into the alley where he punched and kicked him until he was bloody and slumped against a mountain of black bin bags, mewling like a tomcat.

James watched the whole thing, and then he stole back to school, his brain full of fire and his legs wobbling until the blood inside them was cool and strong again. When he thought about following Ransby at the end of the day he kept remembering what he had seen in the alley and went straight home instead.

The next day, after school had finished, James summoned up enough courage to try again.

As Ransby walked he drank two beers, squashing each empty can one-handed and throwing them into the bin, the sunlight running round the wrinkles as each one flew through the air. He kept on going, until the edges of the town became greener and softer, and the buildings fell away and the lane petered out into a track that led to a field. In one corner was a red Ford Granada, its tyres turned to putty in the grass.

James hid behind a patch of brambles, watching Ransby open the driver's door then slam it shut behind him. After getting comfortable in the seat, Ransby gripped the wheel and cranked the gears and pretended to drive somewhere James could not possibly see. But he tried imagining it anyway.

When Ransby clambered out of the car he yawned and burped and walked back through the field and onto the track, until he was just a shape melting into the dust from his footsteps.

James stood beside the car for some time, clenching and

unclenching his fists, whispering words of encouragement until he opened the driver's door. Although the inside smelt fishy and stank of oil, he climbed in slowly and sat behind the wheel. But his stomach shrank when he noticed a large stain on the beige leather of the passenger seat, black at first, then crimson when the sunlight caught it. Tiny pebbles of glass sparkled all around it where the window had smashed leaving just a shark's fin, like a still from a movie.

He fumbled for the door handle and got out and stood beside the car with swallows boomeranging round him as he breathed in the green of the field, trying to forget how the accident had changed everything. Eventually, he started kicking the hours and minutes out of the dandelion heads beside him until they were just empty stalks in the ground, telling himself he was standing somewhere outside time, where the past and present and future meant nothing at all.

But when he turned round and walked back through the field on to the track, the seconds and minutes ticked on again like they always did.

James followed the track to the lane and stopped when he saw Ransby sitting on the verge like a giant toad with a stalk of grass in the corner of his mouth, its feathery end shimmering like a peacock feather.

'All right, goosey?' said Ransby, grinning.

James's breath caught in his throat. He thought about the two boys at school and their broken noses as Ransby stared up at him with two brown unblinking eyes.

'I saw you rescue that bird,' he said quickly, as if it was a magic spell. But Ransby just kept staring. 'It's a robin you know . . . is it ok?' asked James. 'Why did you save it?'

Ransby snipped off the end of the stalk with his teeth then spat it onto the tarmac, making tiny dust motes dance.

'Let's go for a drive,' he growled and stood up and lumbered past James, back towards the field. James didn't know if Ransby's giant body had blocked out the sun or whether it was just a passing cloud, but he felt the sudden chill all the same.

Staring down the lane, James shivered even more as a simple truth inside him brightened: even if he started running, Ransby would catch up with him eventually.

When James opened the car door he glanced at the blood-stain on the seat and Ransby noticed and folded his two broad arms. He stared for a long time as if trying to decide on something, his eyes flicking from the seat to James and back again and, finally, he nodded as if a question had been answered.

'I live in that house you followed me to,' he said. James opened his mouth. Then closed it. Ransby grinned like a fox. 'My nan lives there too. Though she's not living really.' He drummed a big set of fingers on the roof of the car. 'But we're all dying aren't we? From the moment we're born . . . that's what some people say anyway.'

'Do you really think that?'

Ransby nodded and then suddenly he looked tired and his body seemed to shrink slightly, as though someone had opened and closed a valve. 'Do you feel like you're living?'

James just shrugged. He tried not to look at the bloodstain again as he remembered things from the accident, like some sort of dark dream unspooling at the back of his head.

Ransby slammed the driver's door shut and the noise made James flinch. 'How about I show you what else I do,' he said.

And James thought he saw Ransby smile, as if he had known all along about the car and what it would mean to James. And all James could do was smile back, wondering what else he knew.

They clambered up the old stones and sat at the top of the broken windmill where the breeze was gusty and nipped at their ears, forcing them to speak up. As the clouds blew by above them, James watched meadows flashing silver and gold.

Fields of early wheat were cropped low like patches of moss. The single square of ploughed earth he could see looked as soft as velvet.

'Well?' beamed Ransby.

James nodded. 'I go somewhere too.' Ransby listened, waiting for more. 'It's near where I live. The "house on the hill" it's called.'

'Why do you go there?'

'To work out who I'm going to be.'

Ransby nodded like he understood, then mined a nostril for something green and wet and striped a rock beside them with the gloop.

'One day, I'm going to fly out of Falconbury.' He stood up, wobbling as the wind caught his outstretched arms, making James's heart swell, his fingers working like tiny ailerons. 'My nan's the only one keeping me here 'cos she's ill,' he shouted. 'I'll be able to do whatever I want after she's gone. She said I could.'

'What's the matter with her?'

Ransby just shrugged and looked up into the blue sky. The biggest clouds were shaped like giant anvils, sliced shear across their tops, with the smaller ones blowing by like sparks around them.

James closed his eyes and let the wind play over his face. But then he wondered what Ransby really meant, about flying. And when he opened his eyes he panicked when Ransby was no longer there, as if just thinking about it had sent him tumbling over the edge.

But with the wind jammed in his ears like wool, James simply hadn't heard the other boy move further round the wall, and he felt so light for a moment he thought he might blow away in the breeze.

James stood up and raised himself slowly on to his tiptoes, looking down at the ground and thinking about his mother and his stepfather and how life was. When Ransby started yelling and whooping at the sky he looked up.

'We're like each other,' whispered James into the wind, hoping it might carry to someone who cared.

They stayed on the broken windmill for another hour, speaking and laughing, until the wind had rubbed their faces red and it was starting to get cold and the sun had crept close enough to the tops of the trees to turn their twiggy crowns black.

May

When Ransby didn't turn up to school over the next two days, James tried not to think about why. But it was difficult. He kept remembering what Ransby had said. About flying. His mind didn't have its usual spark and school wasn't the same. So he spent a lot of time staring out the window and the teachers ...

     ... just ...

  ... droned.

It was the first time he had ever failed a maths test. But it didn't seem to matter. He saw how school could look through all the other kids' eyes.

Rumours started going round the playground about what had happened to Ransby, but there were so many none of them sounded true. Eventually, at lunchtime on the third day Ransby had been missing, James walked quickly out of the school gates.

He stood on the gravel drive outside Ransby's house for some time, as if listening closely for any clue about what might be happening inside. But all he heard was the distant hum of traffic on the main road a few streets away. The cold was needling his fingertips and the lunch hour was wearing out so he crunched over the gravel towards the front door.

It opened before he got there, and Ransby peered round its edge, blinking in the daylight.

370

Something wasn't right. James was too shocked to know why at first. But then he began to see everything more clearly. Ransby's chin was grazed and mottled with deep greens and mauves. His right cheek was so swollen the eye had disappeared and James could see a black dot shining through the narrow, wrinkled slit. His shaved head was the colour of a windfall plum.

When Ransby moved out from behind the door, James saw a makeshift sling, fashioned from a tea towel, where his right forearm was supposed to be.

'What are you doing here?' whistled Ransby through red, frosted lips and James noticed two empty slots in his bottom row of teeth.

'What happened?' he whispered.

'The drunk bloke from the burger place. Jumped me. With a five iron, I reckon.' Ransby smiled a pink, gummy smile. There were more teeth missing than there should have been. James heard the swish of the golf club in his head and shuddered. 'It's lunchtime,' said Ransby, opening the door wider. 'You must be starving.'

They sat at the kitchen table. On each plate was a mound of mashed potato, surrounded by an oily moat of gravy and peas, with two sausages as big as bananas on top. Ransby swallowed three pink pills with large slurps from a bottle of gin.

'So this is my nan,' gasped Ransby, his breath all fruity and sweet.

James nodded as he looked at the battered bull of a boy and then at his grandmother, and back again.

The old woman didn't seem to hear or even notice James. She was staring at a spot on the table. When she licked her lips and whispered something, James leant closer to try and hear, but she wasn't talking to him.

She was dried out to a wisp in her wheelchair, her cheekbones like tiny elbows at their points with the skin drawn so tight below them he could see the outline of her top teeth, like a row of miniature ribs. Her white downy hair seemed to weigh on her. She was so small and delicate that James imagined her being sucked through the open window at the slightest tug from the breeze, which brushed his face from time to time.

When she grabbed his wrist without warning he flinched. As she looked at him he noticed the mascara on the tips of her eyelashes and the foundation in the pores of her nose. Her finger-nails were so red and lacquered they flashed back the daylight.

He looked at Ransby and the man-boy shrugged. 'She likes to look her best so I make her up. Don't I, Nan? Every morning.' He smoothed down a white tuft of her hair but it sprang up slowly again. 'The last few have taken a bit longer mind.'

'Are you Edmund's friend?' she asked.

James looked at Ransby again.

'I prefer Ted,' he said, as he took another slurp of gin.

'Yes,' replied James, 'I'm his friend.' And he glanced at Ransby but the boy didn't seem to mind what he'd said.

'There's Woolfie,' whispered the old woman, pointing out into the garden. 'Woolfie Saunders.' James could see there was no one there, but he nodded anyway. He scooped up the last of the gravy with his fork and sucked the tines clean to the ends of their silver points and thought about how his mum would never grow old.

'I should get back to school,' he said.

'Can you help me get her up to bed first?' asked Ransby.

James pushed the wheelchair to the bottom of the stairs and then, with Ransby's direction, he helped lift the old woman into the stair lift. She was heavier than she looked, a dead weight slumped in his arms. Her skin smelt of sage and toothpaste.

She could have been ascending into heaven with the sun flashing gold through the window on the landing. As she reached the top the light shone through her hair, making each strand glow, ringing a halo round her fragile head.

'My nan,' mumbled Ransby proudly, through his broken

mouth. And all James could do was nod and think about his mum again.

When he felt a weight on his shoulders he wanted to cry, because it seemed like the whole world was pushing down on him. But then he realised it was Ransby's big arm draped across him. So he smiled and blinked so hard just a single tear swelled out one of his eyes which he wiped away.

The old woman shouted something and waved a hand in the sunshine making the webbing between her fingers shine pink and Ransby burst out laughing and so did James.

When they lifted her into bed she lay breathing heavily, looking up at the ceiling, her hair like foam on the pillow. She gasped like a fish and then closed her eyes, her tiny chest rising and falling, her breath ticking in her throat. She seemed exhausted by the very act of lying there. Of being who she was.

'When she goes, I'll be the only one of my kind left,' said Ransby.

James thought about that. And then he nodded and said, 'I know exactly what you mean.'

Something flickered in the corner of the room, catching his eye, and James beamed when he realised what it was. In a birdcage shaped like a bell the robin was fluttering against the bars, striking musical notes as it touched them.

'Nan kept asking about her budgie,' shrugged Ransby, 'so I managed to put two and two together,' and he grinned.

'I'm glad you did,' said James, smiling back.

'As soon as my nan's gone,' Ransby whispered, 'someone'll have to set that robin free. 'Cos I'll be gone too, as quick as a flash.'

And James nodded and kept staring at the bird, flinching every time it flapped its wings and flew against the bars.

The longer Ransby stayed off school the more all the kids in James's class wondered why, until they started making up stories about him to fill the holes in their heads.

James listened to each one and smiled and told no one the truth.

The teachers didn't seem to mind that Ransby was missing. Or perhaps they didn't care.

He was like a dream that everyone had woken up from.

James held Ransby's secret close. As precious as a pearl in an oyster. Life swilled around him like an ocean . . . his stepfather . . . home . . . school . . . and each lunchtime he went round to the house and helped Ransby with his nan as the man-boy healed, growing stronger again. And it seemed to James that he was healing too, in places that no one could see.

But one Monday, after a weekend of his stepfather, no one answered the doorbell when James rang it. After banging hard on the door he waited for his knuckles to stop burning before flipping the latch on the tall wooden gate at the side of the house and walking down the gravel path into the back garden. He stood listening, staring at four wobbly versions of himself in the glass panes of the conservatory. They vanished like ghosts when he moved and pulled down one white handle and stepped inside.

Shutting the door behind him, the silence was suddenly louder. And so was his heart, which boomed like distant thunder.

'Ransby?'

The fridge clicked on and wobbled making James shudder.

A fly zipped past his nose.

He walked to the edge of the kitchen and peered into the hall.

'Ted?'

He found himself striding quickly to the bottom of the stairs.

The stair lift was at the top. The window on the landing above it dull and grimy, with yellow triangles patched in the corners.

'Hello?' shouted James.

He ran up the stairs and stopped on the landing.

Suddenly, he wasn't sure if he wanted to go any further, so he put his foot down and waited for the sensation to pass.

After taking a breath he started walking towards the old woman's bedroom. He could hear the robin as it pinged and fluttered against the cage and he paused again when he realised his heart was fighting to get out from behind its bars too.

Another fly rose like a zeppelin over his shoulder, so fat and blue that James backed away from the door as the insect disappeared into the bedroom.

He heard a haze of buzzing, made by hundreds of wings, and he put his hand to his nose because suddenly there was a nasty smell.

Slowly, his feet shuffled forward until he was close enough to push the door wider with the tips of his fingers.

He held his breath as he looked over at the bed, his hand over his mouth.

It was stripped back. Crisp white sheets pulled down taut. The pillows plumped. There was nobody there.

No body.

But the flies.

And the smell. Like something rotting in a bin.

James kept his nose covered with a hand.

Through the stench he thought he heard feet tamping down gravel in the drive. Then he heard a key scratching in the front door lock and it seemed that the key was unlocking a chamber in his head too as thoughts tumbled through him.

When the door opened the house seemed to breathe, the sounds of distant traffic blowing in on a draught up the stairs, into the bedroom, scattering flies and making the half-drawn curtains shimmer because the big sash window was open at the bottom, just a slit.

James heard a man laughing outside the front door, then two male voices talking, muffled by the thumping of his heart.

Suddenly, he heard the sound of something else too, in the bedroom with him.

As he turned round he saw it, a dark shape, rising at first. Then a pair of large wings flapping as the bird crash-landed on the chest of drawers, sliding across the top as its black talons struggled to catch hold.

James kept quite still.

He knew it was a buzzard perched in front of him, with feathers a hundred different shades of brown and amber eyes shot clean through the middle, but he couldn't understand why it was in the room. There was blood on the hook of its black beak, a red crust on the yellow leather of its snout.

James looked down and saw a plate broken into two pieces on the floor, the remnants of a serving of stew around it. Beside the congealed mess, a dead rat, its head picked open, flies settling on it like cinders.

James could just hear the men's voices at the bottom of the stairs.

'You say the boy left a note?'

The buzzard hopped and flapped on top of the chest of drawers, panting as it flexed its wings. Inside the confined space of the bedroom it seemed huge. Prehistoric.

'Said he was done with the world like his gran.'

'Who found the old woman's body?'

'Neighbours. Over the weekend.'

A door downstairs opened then clunked shut a moment later, like a guillotine cutting both heads from their bodies. In the silence, James was thinking hard about who the voices belonged to and about the words he had heard. But the memory of them already seemed jumbled up and difficult to decipher. All he could hear was Ransby's voice as if the boy was speaking through the walls.

'Cos I'll be gone too as quick as a flash.

Suddenly James wanted to be sick. The smell in the room seemed to have talons hooked into the clean pink inside of his throat.

The buzzard shifted its tail feathers and sprayed a foul

376

white stripe against the wall. The bird was panting harder, its set of clear eyelids opening and closing like a toad's.

The sounds of muffled voices and footsteps filtered up through the bones of the house.

James stared at the buzzard and it stared straight back. And all the time the robin in the cage was tugging at the bars.

As the curtains moved again, James wondered about the window being slightly open and the voices and the buzzard and the rat and the plate and Ransby and his nan and the note. They were like jigsaw pieces in a box. But none of them made sense, however much he fumbled with them. There was no picture.

Someone'll have to set that robin free. 'Cos I'll be gone too as quick as a flash.

James found himself edging towards the curtains, watching the buzzard all the time, wary of its beak and feet. Finally, he slipped his fingers under the bottom section of the window and tugged it as high as it would go.

He felt the weight of a shadow above him.

A hiss.

The smell of the wild.

The buzzard flapped its wings once as it skimmed low across the garden. Then, like a giant bat, it swooped up between two houses and disappeared before swinging into view again, circling higher and higher as if the weak spring sun was sucking it upwards.

When the two men opened the conservatory doors and emerged into the garden, James shrank back from the window and their conversation about the house and what needed to be done to it.

He picked up the cage by its metal ring and it swung in his fingers as he crept down the stairs, the robin holding on tight to the bars, birdseed spraying on to the carpet.

He walked quickly until he was in a different street. When he found an alley he sat down and cried into his arms because nothing in the old woman's bedroom made sense even though he had been a part of it.

When his shirt sleeves were sodden he wiped his eyes and stood up and checked his watch. He decided there was just enough time.

As he walked quickly through the streets the robin blinked at the world outside the cage, trilling notes as sharp as glass. Eventually, he left the town behind.

From the top of the old windmill, James looked out at the fields below and nodded although he wasn't sure why. It was just a feeling that someone might be watching.

Then he pulled up the clasp on the tiny door and held up the cage. The robin warbled, its tiny black eyes shining. Slowly it hopped forwards and fluttered clean out of the cage, landing on the tumbledown wall of the windmill, where it wiped its tiny brown beak as if sharpening a knife. Then it flicked up into the air, rising and falling, bouncing on the breeze, and not looking back.

As James watched the horizon swallow it up he thought about Ransby and where he might be. And then he climbed down again out of the wind.

Later that day at school there was an announcement. Edmund Ransby had disappeared because he had been upset about his grandmother dying. He had left a suicide note but the police were still looking for him and when the teacher asked if anyone knew anything everybody shook their heads, even James.

The teacher told them to pray, saying that if anyone wanted to speak about anything they could.

But no one did.

Some kids said Ransby's body had been swept out to sea because he had put stones in his pocket and waded into the river. They said this because his note had been left on a tree beside the riverbank skewered by a knife, his shoes below it.

But Ransby had apparently died in other ways too. Some kids thought he was alive but they didn't know where and they couldn't say why.

James didn't know what to believe. Whenever he remembered the buzzard in the bedroom or the robin and how he had set it free he began to feel a flutter in his chest. And sometimes he looked up and saw Ransby peering round a corner at him, following him just like James had done. But he knew in his heart it wasn't real. James told himself that whatever Ransby had done it was because he had wanted to do it. And the more James thought about that, the more he went to the house on the hill to sit on the old sofa, working out how he was going to do what he wanted too.

June

After school it's the same routine every day. James changes out of his uniform and avoids his stepfather by escaping to the house on the hill, to be with his secrets chalked up on the wall.

But today is different.

James comes thumping down the stairs and his stepfather is there in the kitchen, home early from work. There's a fug about him, sweet as sugar, and when the man burps, James knows he's been drinking.

As he moves for the backdoor his stepfather watches, like something hunting its prey.

James pauses as soon as he sees the pile of post on the table. There's a postcard on top, a picture of a robin, standing in the snow with its head cocked looking up out of the picture.

'Tea,' growls his stepfather, pointing at the kettle on the cooker.

James nods and sparks a blue ring on the hob, then grabs a mug and drops in a teabag, which seems to fall for minutes before it hits the bottom. Or at least that's how it feels as he wonders about the postcard and who it's for, and who it's from.

When he hears a gentle snoring, he holds his breath and turns round to see his stepfather's chin resting on his chest, his eyes closed.

Quietly, James picks up the postcard and checks the back. There's his name and address on one half and a single word on the other. Another name.

Ted

As soon as he smiles, the kettle starts to whistle and James plants the postcard straight back down on the pile before his stepfather can see too much through his bleary eyes as he lifts his head.

The hot water turns brown in an instant, the steam from the mug misting James's face as he lets the bag stew. When he opens the fridge, he blinks at the bright white chill, hunting for the milk bottle with his hand. It's colder than stone when he plucks it from the rack beside the orange juice. Greasy too.

Above the whirr of the fridge and the hum of his heart he hears another noise, the sound of something being torn up.

When he whips round it seems to be snowing for an instant until he tells himself the truth, that it's tiny pieces of the postcard fluttering to the floor. And then his stepfather lunges for the milk bottle, screaming about something as he grabs it, then gasping as it slips from his hand.

When it breaks on the floor, James's heart breaks too. Again. Because he knows what's coming.

He watches the milk funneling through the grooves between the tiles, trying to tune out his stepfather's rants and hollers.

But the punch on his arm breaks his trance. And then he hears a word bright as a shooting star inside him.

It's Ransby's voice shouting . . .

Run.